MANHATTAN NORTH

By MARTHA ALBRAND

Under CHRISTINE LAMBERT

Manhattan North

MARTHA ALBRAND

COWARD, McCANN & GEOGHEGAN, INC.
New York

MANHATTAN NORTH

CHAPTER

ONE

THERE WAS NO WIND THAT NIGHT. The snow fell softly and quietly, settling quickly on the bare branches of the trees and on the ground. A tall, rather slender man, holding himself very erect, stood waiting for the light to change before he crossed Fifth Avenue slowly toward the entrance to Central Park between Seventy-sixth and Seventy-seventh streets.

It was ten minutes to eight, and except for frequent buses, a few taxis, and private cars, the street was deserted. In this neighborhood, people were either at dinner or had already left their homes for the theater, the opera, or private parties. In spite of the emptiness around him, the man stopped every few paces as if he wanted to make certain nobody was watching him, turning his head first to the left, then to the right, before entering the park. But then, instead of walking straight on into the lighted circle of sparsely placed lanterns, he stepped rapidly to the right, and between some low bushes and frail trees that grew parallel to the wall, separating the city from its cherished spot of open sky and nature, zipped open his pants.

While he was relieving himself, another, slighter man came running up to him with a speed that was almost inhuman, and plunged a knife between the shoulders of the tall man, who, with not even enough breath left to scream fell with a heavy thud face down into the soft, dry snow.

The killer, apparently in no particular hurry, drew out his knife, and held it in his hands for a moment. Then he turned the body around, bent over it, after which he pushed the knife up his dark, woolen sweater and walked away slowly, lighting a cigarette as he reached the park entrance. He was in no way aware that he had just murdered a Justice of the Supreme Court of the United States.

CHAPTER

TWO

I NEVER WANTED TO STUDY LAW, and certainly not to join a corporate law firm, but I did both under the pressure of sentimentality. Death, according to San Angelo, my father's partner, brought obligations with it, so when my parents were killed in an airplane accident over Portugal, he took me in—an uncle somewhere in San Francisco was only too glad when I begged to stay with my godfather— and I grew up under San Angelo's influence. When the time came, I took his advice, as usual, and enrolled in Columbia's Law School. I became editor-in-chief of the *Columbia Law Review*, an honor, certainly, and San Angelo was overjoyed. After my bar examination he had his way once more—no "poor law" for me, no civil rights, no criminal defense, but my place in the firm my great-grandfather had founded. Yes, sentimentality again, augmented this time by the fact that Justo, San Angelo's son, a few years my senior and my "ideal image," was going to come in at the same time.

I thought of all this as I made my way past the library, through the long corridors, to San Angelo's office. The whole floor sparkled with modernism. Saarinen chairs, desks with everything built in, for decoration a few Arps, no copies, an

Epstein bust, a Chagall—a red cow flying and an angel sitting—until you opened one of the soundproof doors and
stood, taken aback. Old-fashioned, deep, worn, brown
leather chairs, genuine leather, a couch on which one could
take a nap, a screen with a washbasin behind it, a spitoon on
the floor next to a desk littered with papers, heavily lined
curtains instead of shades, and over everything the smog of
cold cigars.

"Fine," said San Angelo, as if I'd already asked how he
felt, and scratched his head the way monkeys cautiously
approach an itching spot. As a matter of fact, he was called
"the old monkey" by everybody in the office, affectionately
but with great respect. No other name could have been
more descriptive. Even his walk, the way he lumbered
along, reminded one of an ape. But it was his eyes that
startled you most with their deep melancholy, which
seemed in conflict with their alertness. Most people though
called him by the first half of his last name, "San," since he
hated the name his parents had chosen for their oldest son—
Ambrosio. Otherwise he was as Italian as they come, small,
wiry, a body in constant motion, in a suit and tie that betrayed the vainness of Latin men. I glanced away from him,
to the couch, above which hung a portrait of my father, his
name attached to the lower end of the gold frame: Thaddeus J. Wood. I had never been able to figure out how those
two men had become friends, and finally partners, men from
different continents, background, class. There were stories,
of course, told over and over *ad nauseam*, none of them
quite convincing and all of them, I thought, romanticized.

"Heard?" said San Angelo, only it wasn't a question. He
always took for granted that one knew what he was talking
about. "I must say I couldn't be happier that for once our
lethargic population is stirring in its sleep." He had an impressive voice, clear, well-modulated, resonant. Even in excitement it never reached that shrill pitch which grates on
the nerves. He was referring to the assassination of Justice

Butworth which had stunned the nation, and for more than a week now had made headlines in the newspapers, been commented on endlessly by radio and television reporters, and had caused a wave of anger and fear. Everybody was speculating about the motive. The general assumption tended to take political reasons for granted. A couple of weeks before his death the Justice had upheld the law against obscenity. Suddenly it was recalled that there had been quite a reaction to his decision. The editor of a small paper, apparently the mouthpiece of a lunatic fringe group somewhere in the Middle West, had attacked Butworth and demanded his impeachment. Other papers had picked up the vicious article, pointing out the dangers of such attacks and demands merely because a handful of people didn't like a decision of the Supreme Court. The furor had mounted, nourished undoubtedly by the fact that no trace of the killer or anyone associated with him had been uncovered. Somehow, since Butworth had been a crony of the President and often acted as his adviser, it had been taken for granted that the killer would be speedily apprehended.

"A commission is to be appointed," San Angelo said, "by the President, to investigate the Effect of Violence on the Judiciary and Terror as a Measure of Influencing Judicial Decisions." He sounded as content as if the commission had been his personal suggestion. He had been deeply upset by this latest act of violence; besides, he had known the Justice personally.

I shrugged. I didn't think much of commissions. They rarely got at the truth of the matter, and if they did, it was ignored. I said so. San Angelo held a fresh cigar to his large ear and listened intently to the almost inaudible sound of the wrapping, which would tell him if it was too dry or still wet enough. "That's a pity," he said. "I thought you'd jump at it."

At a loss, I asked, "Jump at what?"

"Our office," he said, stretching his words with satisfac-

tion, "was asked if we could spare a bright young fellow."
He grinned. More than anyone else, he knew how bored I
was with the endless grind of contracts, memoranda affida-
vits, prolonged and sterile discussions and arguments. Yet
until now it had been he who had prevented me from taking
as much time as I would have liked for outside work,
scoffing when I told him I wanted to join the Council of
New York Associates. After a year or more of arguments, I'd
grown tired of repeating that many other firms gave their
younger associates a chance to do *pro bono* work, only to be
told that if that was the way I felt, I might as well leave. Yet
how could I leave without letting it come to a final break
between us, and this I didn't want. So I spent a couple of
evenings working on public-interest cases, holding lectures,
helping to organize meetings, advising people who couldn't
afford a lawyer and had very little idea about their rights as
citizens. This assignment, although it wasn't exactly what
I'd been looking for, was a chance of getting out of the rut
for a while, and I found myself wishing suddenly that it
would take months. "Thank you," I said.

"Two days a week," said San Angelo, and anticipating my
question, "no, not Washington. Here. You can't be spared
altogether, nor can everybody move to Washington for
whatever time it may take to come to a conclusion. I don't
know what the setup's going to be, but I guess it'll be the
usual thing—some big shot for chairman, staff directors,
liaison, a galaxy of brains—sociologists, psychiatrists, criminologists, what have you." He smiled again. "And with
pay."

"That's good," I said.

He blew a cloud of smoke into my face. "There was a time
when you'd have done it for nothing."

"You cured me of idealism."

"Did I?" he said. "I hope not. I hope there are some ves-
tiges left, I really do."

CHAPTER

THREE

HOME WAS A GROUND-FLOOR APARTMENT on West Tenth Street. I considered myself lucky to have found it. The entrance wasn't exactly impressive. The door opened onto a narrow, dark corridor with insufficient closet space, an always cold and rather primitive john that could be warmed only by an electric stove, a bathtub which must have been manufactured for midgets, and a gas heater that worked poorly. Next to it, an uncomfortable, small, windowless kitchen, but the sliding door at the far end of the passage opened into a two-story-high studio. It had huge windows on either side, although one was actually a glass door, leading to a twenty by thirty stone-walled garden. Up a rather steep staircase there was a balcony, partly open, but closed where the bedroom was located. A black woman, who had been with the former owner, had agreed to stay on if she could have things her way, which meant she'd come in to clean when it suited her. When she was in a good mood, she'd leave something in the ice box for me to warm up.

Tiger greeted me with his joyous bark, getting up on his hind legs and licking the side of my neck. He was a mutt, half Shepherd, half Chow, with a heavy coat of beige-black hair and an ink-black tongue.

"Down, down," I said. "That's enough now. Stop it," before I said hello to Susanne. She was sitting in front of the
fireplace on a little Moroccan taboret, made of different colored patches of leather, which I had brought back with me
a couple of years ago, warming her hands against the flames.
Her hands were nice, slim, long-fingered, and knowing.
We'd been together now for over four years. She lived
around the corner, on Fifth Avenue. If she finished early,
she would pop in on the evenings we had set aside for ourselves, three times a week, instead of waiting for me to pick
her up. "I'll just wash up," I told her, and she nodded without answering. But when I came back a few minutes later,
she rose and put her arms around me. She was almost as tall
as I, and she removed my glasses, a thing she always did
because she said they were in the way for the kind of kissing
she liked. Our lips had barely touched though, when she let
me go abruptly. "What's the matter?"

"Nothing. Why?"

"You're distracted," she said. "Anything wrong?"

I poured her a gin, with a drop of Angostura, and myself a
Jack Daniels from the tray she had brought in before I arrived, bottles, glasses, ice and all, even some nuts. Usually
she wasn't that housewifely but let me wait on her. She took
a sip, then threw back her head so that her long black hair
bobbed on her shoulders and back. "What is it?"

"Nothing," I said. I hadn't been aware of anything different in the way I'd taken her in my arms, yet she was right,
as usual, a fact which sometimes annoyed me. On my way
home from the office I hadn't been thinking of meeting her,
but only about my assignment on the Presidential committee. I told her about it.

"That's fine," she said, "just fine," but it didn't sound con-
gratulatory.

"I thought you'd be glad to see me get off the treadmill, at
least for a while."

"I am," she said, sitting down on the couch and pulling up
her legs, which were long and slim like her hands, and quite

exciting in their silky black stockings. "I'm glad for you, but where does that leave me? You'll be busier than ever, the way I know you, throwing yourself body and soul into this new job, and the trip to Washington is tiring."

"Not Washington," I said. "I'll be given an office here, in some government building or post office, wherever they can find room for me."

That calmed her a little. "But you'll meet people who are much more interesting than me, people you can talk to about all the things that bore me."

"Even if I do, I'll keep our evenings free. That's a promise."

"Mighty handsome of you," she said. "Three evenings a week. Sometimes you make me feel like a call girl."

It was my turn to ask, "What's the matter?"

She poured herself another drink. "You really don't know, do you?"

"Know what?"

"Don't be stupid, Tad. Or do you really think a woman can be content with so little time."

"It's all the time I have."

"It's all the time you want to have for me. Hardly ever lunch, never a few hours of shopping. When have you ever come with me to pick out a dress? And your weekends— they're all reserved for your damn San Angelo."

Actually she wasn't exaggerating. I really did spend nearly all my weekends with San Angelo at his place in Connecticut.

"Sometimes I wonder if the two of you aren't having an affair."

I glared at her, then found it funny and laughed. "Susy, don't be ridiculous. You know what the guy means to me. He . . ."

Susanne covered her ears. "Don't tell me. I don't want to hear about it. He took your father's place, yes, yes, and you grew up in his house, and Justo . . . if I have to listen to you explain it all once more, I'll throw up."

I lighted a cigarette, something I usually did when I
didn't know what to say and was too nervous to get out my
pipe and go through the whole ritual of filling and lighting
it.

"And that poor child," she went on. "Melinda needs me. I
promised Justo . . . blah, blah, blah. I need you too."

I was afraid she was going to cry and sat down next to
her. It was a mistake. With a shoulder to lean on the tears
began to flow. "Hush, Susy, hush."

"I'm not Melinda. I need something a lot better than
that."

"Then come out to Ridgefield with me next Saturday."

She shook her head vehemently.

"Why not? He's invited you often enough."

She drew away from me and sat up straight. "Haven't you
grasped yet that he hates me?"

"Oh, Lord," I said, suddenly impatient. "Do we have to go
through all that again? How often must I tell you that after
it happened, yes, he didn't care to see you, but since
then . . ."

Susanne had been driving the car when a trailer truck had
jumped the median and crashed into us. Miraculously she
had been scarcely hurt. I had suffered a nasty head wound
which had left my right eye with almost no vision, but
Justo, San Angelo's son, and Clarissa, his wife, had died a
few days later. "He knows as well as you and I that it wasn't
your fault, that nobody could have done anything different."

"I tell you, he hates me."

"Come out with me and you'll see that whatever he may
have felt or said in a moment of hysteria didn't last longer
than those first terrible minutes when he was told . . ."

"Besides, he's jealous of me."

"Rubbish!"

"You know what he's hoping and why he keeps telling you
how dependent Melinda is on you?" She took a deep breath.
"He hopes you'll marry her."

I couldn't help laughing. "You're nuts! Melinda is . . . let's see. How old? Twelve. I'm twenty-nine. There's a difference of seventeen years. Nobody in his right mind would expect a man to wait six years for a wife, nor would San Angelo want his granddaughter to marry a man that much older. You're nuts, Susy. You're out of your mind."

I got up and turned on the radio to get the seven o'clock news. A fire in New Jersey had killed three members of one family, students had demonstrated in Utah, the housing committee . . . no trace yet of the killer of Justice Butworth. The stock exchange was down again. A cold wave was threatening New York. Temperatures would fall to below twenty. Light snow was expected. Sports.

I went back to the couch. She had stretched out on it, taking most of the room, her hands folded across her breasts as if to immobilize them under her tight, black silk jersey. She was staring up at the skylight and barely moved to make room for me. I fixed myself another Jack Daniels and stroked her legs absentmindedly. No trace of the killer. Would he ever be found? Had the Justice been murdered because he had upheld the law against obscenity? How big a part did judicial decisions play in such acts of violence? The commission was a sound idea.

"Tad." Susanne's voice was flat, so it failed to warn me. "Marry me."

It came so unexpectedly, I was stunned. We had never discussed marriage. She wasn't a girl—at least, so I thought —who wanted to get married, as a matter of fact it had been one of her greatest charms that she had always made light of any deeper commitment. And it had never occurred to me to attach myself to anyone. I didn't know what to say. I felt ten years old and helpless, and I grinned with embarrassment. "I'm not joking," she said.

I looked at her. She was beautiful. She was good company and wonderful in bed. But did I want to marry her?

"In all honesty, I've never thought about marriage."

"Then it's time you did."

"Well . . . I'm flattered."

"Come off it, Tad," she said, with the sweetest smile. "Think it over but don't think too long."

I got up and threw a log on the fire, which didn't need it. Think. Think of giving this girl a claim on me. On my life, on my time, on my thoughts, my chances. Marriage was a contract. Did I want Susanne for a partner? Did I want to see her every morning when I woke up, every night when I went to bed? Compromise with her whims, her status as my wife?

"We're getting along so beautifully . . ."

"You are. I'm not. I'm doing a boring job, day in, day out, and I'm a perfectly normal creature. I want a man, a home, and a child."

"You never said so before."

"I don't like to rush into things. But we've been together four years, and as far as I'm concerned, that's it. Or do *you* still need more time?" She spoke lightly. "Maybe you're taking San Angelo as an example. Because he married late . . ." She waved at me not to interrupt her. "I know. He had five sisters who had to get married first, and two younger brothers to set up in business, but you have no one to take care of, no responsibilities, no considerations. Tad, I know it's only San Angelo's influence that you've stayed a bachelor this long."

"Leave San Angelo out of this. He's never interfered with my private life."

"You forget that you told me that when you were twenty-two there was a girl, her name was Irene . . ."

She was right. I had forgotten about Irene, and that San Angelo had said, when I confessed I was in love and wanted to marry her, that I was too young to tie myself down but should wait and see how often I'd be in love before I really was. "Respect is more important than love," he had impressed on me. "Love, sex—wonderful—but what really counts is respect for the other person, affection that isn't based on emotions, an understanding of the other's needs above and beyond one's own desires—those are the pillars on which a successful marriage rests."

I stared into the flames. What was I? The product of the philosophies of others with none as yet formed by myself?

"I'd never fight a divorce," said Susanne, "if it didn't work out."

I felt such pity for her then, I almost said, "All right. Why not? Let's try." But something held me back, some Utopian vision that there had to be a woman, somewhere, not more beautiful nor more satisfactory than Susanne, but . . .

An embarrassing silence grew between us. Finally I managed to say, not lightly but with a deeply felt seriousness, "I don't want to lose you."

"But you also don't want to marry me."

She was laughing, laughing at herself and her lost battle. "Come on, pour me a last drink and don't look so crestfallen. You'll get over me and I'll get over you. One always does, doesn't one? If one lets enough time go by."

She held up her glass to me in a toast. There was a small indentation on her chin; I had often caressed it. "I see no reason for splitting up so abruptly."

"But I do," she said, and cracked a nut between her teeth. "I'm quite an old lady. Twenty-seven. With not a lot of time left to invest myself without success. I want children and I want them while I'm still young enough to enjoy them."

I was grateful to her for swallowing the bitterness she must have felt, for not telling me what a bastard I was, wanting her yet not wanting her enough. She even had enough sensitivity not to force a last kiss. She got her coat while I thought she'd merely gone to the john, and came back into the room all wrapped up, with the funny little stocking-cap she preferred to a scarf or hat, and put the key to my apartment on the table between fireplace and couch. "It was fun, wasn't it, Tad?" she said. "Good night. Take care."

I didn't open the door for her, something I'd always done, no matter how tired; it closed softly, and I was alone. After a while I went into the kitchen. Rose had left a nicely browned, whole chicken, a mixed salad, and half an apple pie she must have baked at home. I found I wasn't hungry and went back into the studio. I poured myself another drink and took out my pipe and the little leather bag with my special mixture of tobacco. I went over to my writing desk which stood at an angle with the French window. Tiger came downstairs, his nails making the scratching noise on the uncarpeted wood that had always irritated Susanne. His nails couldn't be cut because the bloodline went up all the way. He put his head on my knee, reminding me that I had forgotten to take him out. I didn't feel like getting up and just reached around and opened the window. He rushed out, and an icy gust of cold air hit my back. I didn't give him much time before I whistled him back in. He went straight to the fireplace and lay down in front of it instead of running upstairs and into his basket in my bedroom. I took out a sheet of writing paper and put it in my typewriter, then took it out again and groped for a pen. "Susy," I wrote, then my glance fell on the photos I had out—my parents, San Angelo, his granddaughter, Melinda. I hadn't seen the child for at least twelve days. I looked at them all, but I looked longest at San Angelo. There were people who could dominate others by some sort of emanation. I had never believed in such mysterious forces.

I put the picture in the lowest drawer of my desk where I kept other photos taken throughout the years. I didn't write the letter to Susanne. There was really nothing I could say. Unless I was ready to tell her I wanted to marry her. I went back to the couch and stretched out on it. Where her head had rested, I could smell her perfume. Chanel No. 5. Or Arpége. I couldn't remember which one I'd brought back to her from Paris. As I lay there watching the fire die, I became aware of the cold the newscaster had predicted. The heating had gone off, there was a draft from where pane joined frame. Susy had always said that all the colds she suffered during the winter came from the draft in my apartment, and that one would have to move into the fire-place to keep warm.

CHAPTER

FOUR

I WAS GIVEN AN OFFICE on Foley Square. Way downtown. In the United States Court House. You had to have an identification card, and the two policemen who sat at a table in a roped-off space on the ground floor, opposite the heavy entrance door, checked it. First one, then the other. They were husky fellows, almost bursting out of their uniforms, and they looked like twins. Both rosy-cheeked and fat with inertia. They had big, round, forget-me-not blue eyes and small, cruel lips that closed over excellent teeth. They were suspicious of me and I didn't like them, but like everybody else in the building I was soon calling them Mike and Pete.

The office was on the third floor. It must have been a coat room once, or some sort of storage place, it was that small. There were two desks—one for me, one for a secretary, hers with a typewriter, mine bare. A plant stood on the window-sill, one of those cactuses that grow whether you look after it or not. A water container was fastened to the wall, behind my desk. I was constantly bumping my head against the faucet. Whenever Mrs. Johnson wanted a drink, she had to ask me to give it to her because there wasn't room to get to it when I was at my desk.

24

She was a huge woman. Her hair was thin and oily and at times smelled badly from the stuff she used on several bald spots. Her nose dripped, a sinus condition, she explained, and she liked to clean her ears with Q-tips. She introduced herself as Mrs. Johnson, but in my mind I always called her Miss Johnson because I couldn't imagine anyone ever having wanted to marry her. She was the most efficient secretary I had ever come across and without her I would have been lost. She didn't seem to mind the peeling walls, once painted Williamsburg green but gray now with dirt, dead bugs, and graffiti scrawled across them, nor that the filing cabinet was either so stuck, you had to call in the handy man, or stayed open in spite of our combined efforts to close it, so the handyman had to be called in again. And of course had to be tipped every time. There were two telephones. She kept hers constantly busy—perhaps she felt that telephones which weren't being used were a waste—mine hardly rang more than three times a day.

The first morning she placed a bundle of clippings on my none too steady desk. "I went to the library to get them. Thought you might want to inform yourself again on everything published about this latest act of violence."

Again I read the facts I knew already. Justice Butworth's body had been discovered by a dogwalker. At about six in the morning. One of the dogs, a setter, had been let loose, although this was against the rules of the dogwalkers as well as of the park department. The dog had not obeyed the whistle that had called him back to leash but, howling with excitement, had gone on scratching in a snow pile. The boy, a certain Percy Maggin, had been forced to cross over to the underbrush near the stone wall. By the time he'd got there, the dog had scraped away enough snow to reveal the face of a dead man. Maggin had known better than to touch the body and had hurried out of the park, looking for police. Finding no cop at this early hour, he had tried one of the public phone booths. It was out of order. So was the one

three blocks up, after which he was out of change. He'd
decided to give up, when he had spotted a police car and
succeeded in stopping it. In an interview he said he wished
he hadn't bothered. Although all he had done was tell the
officers they'd better have a look at a heap of snow about
thirty yards from the Seventy-sixth Street entrance to the
park, the car had picked him up a while later at one of the
houses on Madison Avenue where he was delivering two of
his charges. He had been pulled in and interrogated and,
since it was obvious that he had nothing to do with the
murder, had been released two hours later. But by that time
he had missed two lectures at Columbia and was furious.

Only at the morgue, in the Chief Medical Examiner's
office had the corpse been identified. Butworth had been
stabbed. Once. The knife or stiletto had pierced the right
ventricle of the heart. He had been dead, according to the
medical examiner's report, about ten hours at the most. No
weapon had been found, no witness discovered, nobody had
been noticed by any of the park department employees. Nor
had there been any identification on the body, no driver's
license, diner's card, not even visiting cards in the expensive
black leather wallet which had not been disturbed and still
contained one hundred and fifty dollars in twenties, tens,
and fives.

Mrs. Butworth, upon being notified, had gone into shock,
but her daughter, about whom I hadn't heard before, had
readily answered whatever questions had been put to her.
Her poise and clarity were praised by a Washington re-
porter. To one of the many inquiries—why had the Justice
been in New York—she had answered that he had been an
opera buff, and in the habit of going to Lincoln Center
whenever he could get away for the weekend. That night he
had intended to hear *Fidelio*. Her mother considered opera
a bastard art or, according to another account, wasn't musi-
cal, besides she didn't like New York, but the Justice's
daughter had sometimes accompanied him. She didn't know

any friends or acquaintances he might have visited in that
area, but of course there might have been people he'd
dropped in on, for a drink or an early dinner. He usually
stayed at the Plaza and had a snack in the Oak Room or the
Oyster Bar before going to bed. Her testimony was not cor-
roborated by the management of the Plaza. There was no
record of Justice Butworth ever having stayed there. Perhaps he had used a different name to avoid publicity.

"I didn't like him," said Mrs. Johnson. "As a matter of fact
I was furious when his appointment went through."

I said nothing, although I, too, had been dismayed, two
years ago, when Clark Jameson Butworth had been appointed to the Supreme Court. In my eyes his record was far
from distinguished. He came from the South where he had
managed fairly successfully to fight desegregation, had been
a member of some very rightest societies in his youth, and
his decisions as circuit judge in the court of appeals had
been questionable, to say the least. He was in contempt of
all students, if not of the entire youth of America, and had
been fond of starting and ending his banal speeches with a
proclamation for law and order as the only salvation. To me
he had always seemed to be a man whose capacities didn't
suffice for the demands made on him professionally. A harassed man. Still, he had been appointed. For life.

For years San Angelo and I had had a standing debate
about the organization of the Supreme Court. In my opinion, nine men with such all-embracing power, responsible to
no one, should not be appointed for life. San Angelo didn't
agree. My dislike of Butworth, however, and my uneasiness
when faced with this sort of mentality, had nothing to do
with my strong feelings that neither he nor I should be
murdered for our views.

Shortly before noon, Dermot, my staff director, stuck his
head in the door. He had called me the night before to give
me the address of my office. The commission was being di-
vided into twelve separate areas, each headed by a distin-

guished lawyer, and a historian, to go through files in every
state and ferret out any possible evidence of cases where
terror had influenced the judiciary. At the same time ex-
amples in foreign countries had to be found for comparisons
and conclusions. Psychiatrists, criminologists, experts on social issues were to be called in, analysts of poverty and sociologists. My job was to serve as liaison for the eastern area,
with a legal perspective on whatever our men produced.
Also I had to find an editor to put the material together.

Mrs. Johnson got up tactfully and left the room, and
Dermot sat down in her chair. He was a rather small man
with a head too big for his body, bigger now since he had let
his hair grow. He had been one of my teachers at Columbia
and a friend of San Angelo's. He drew one finger across the
wall next to him. It came away dirty. He shook his head.
"Not much of a pad, but I'm glad San Angelo could spare
you, Tad."

It was flattering that he should remember my name. "I'd
appreciate it," I said, "if you'd give me a rundown of exactly
what I'm supposed to do."

"Confer with consultants. Ask the experts to get new
angles on this or that. Read their analyses, coordinate, elim-
inate what's repetitious, get things to the different depart-
ments. If you aren't familiar with the data the Leiden Group
collected, or the Robert Winslow Study on Social Integra-
tion, Suicide and Homicide, or the Feierabend Report, I'd
advise you to have a look at them. It will help you avoid
much unnecessary work. You're more or less free to assign
people to certain tasks." He handed me a list. "Here's something to start with."

"But can anything constructive come of it?"

"A viable conclusion?" He pursed his lips. "I doubt it. But
that's no reason not to try. We may come across some ele-
ments that could help us on the road toward such a conclusion. The Butworth murder, for instance—will it affect the
judicial system? And how? But we always have to keep in

mind that violence is not a new manifestation; it's an inbuilt characteristic of our nation. You'll find that we have more assassinations than you may have realized. Senators, Congressmen, judges, governors, minor officials—to say nothing of four Presidents—have been assassinated since this nation was founded. We rank—you may know it or not—as one of the most unstable nations in the world. The point is—how much are our courts influenced by all this?"

He rose, stretched himself, or perhaps he was standing on tiptoe to lend his words emphasis. "Got to run. Call on me if something comes up that you'd like advice on or just want to talk over. Good luck."

A little while after he had left, I went out to get some lunch.

Foley Square is not a square, but rather a misshapen triangle, with benches and a few trees, even some low hedges. Now it was almost black with people. Like waves they rolled out of the giant Federal Office Building, which the windows of my office faced, the Justice Department, the United States Custom Court, the County Court House, from the Motor Vehicle Bureau down the street and the subway station. They scattered in every direction. In spite of the cold, the green benches were occupied by people eating the lunch they'd brought with them. I walked down Pearl Street and around the corner, but every Chinese restaurant had a line. I retraced my steps, stopped at a cafeteria and at a hamburger place opposite without even being able to get a cup of coffee. After half an hour I gave up and went back to my office, hungry and bad-tempered. But lo and behold, on my desk stood a paper cup with coffee, still boiling hot, an envelope with nonfattening sugar and a roast beef sandwich with two sweet-sour gherkins wrapped in wax paper. On top of it lay the bill. A dollar ninety-five. Outrageous, but I'd have paid more gladly. I wolfed it down.

"You're an angel," I told Mrs. Johnson when she came back. "How did you know..."

"It'll take you a little time to get known around here." She smiled. "But as long as they regard you as a tourist, I'll be happy to take care of your lunch. And now let me have your list of the people you want to work with or contact. You don't have to dictate the letters, I mean introducing yourself, and so on, if you have something more important to do."

CHAPTER

FIVE

A s usual, I took a taxi instead of the bus on Friday
morning, to get Tiger and my suitcase to the office on
Fifth Avenue and Forty-fourth Street, where Wood,
San Angelo and Benson was located on the twenty-sixth
floor. I didn't see San Angelo during the day, but shortly
after four, his secretary rang me. "Mr. San Angelo wants
me to let you know he'll be ready to leave in ten minutes."

I thanked her, wished her a good weekend, cleared my
desk, grabbed my suitcase and briefcase and a book I'd
bought earlier that morning, and made my way to the elevator. San Angelo's black Cadillac was waiting at the curb.
Riley, San Angelo's chauffeur, opened the door for me. He
was a huge Irishman who looked more like a lumberjack,
used to a rugged outdoor life, than a valet, butler, or driver,
all of which duties he had to perform and sometimes resented. Tiger, of course, jumped into the car first, pushing
against Mrs. Riley's hat, which made her grunt with disgust.
She always wore a hat, even when all she had to do was mail
a letter at the corner. Her small face looked like the inside
of a lemon with all the juice squeezed out, and her eyes were
a watery blue. She was the worst-tempered woman I'd ever
met but the world's best cook. She held a half-open basket

31

on her lap. Her two cats were fast asleep; they had already
been given a tranquilizer for the almost two-hour ride to
Ridgefield. Between her and the wheel sat Melinda. She was
asleep too. Her head had slipped down the black leather
upholstery, and she didn't open her eyes when I playfully
pulled one of her long, thick, carrot-red braids.

Usually there would have been another passenger—Doug
Farmer, one of Melinda's boyfriends. He lived next to the
house on Seventy-seventh Street, and I thought him by far
the nicest of her pals. A little too old though, if one wanted
to be critical. Not many sixteen-year-old boys cared for a
girl Melinda's age. But then, Melinda excelled at tennis, his
favorite game, and they used to win all the tournaments in
their class, one of the few social occasions for youngsters in
our part of Connecticut.

From the back seat San Angelo said impatiently, "Get in,"
and when I did, he introduced the person seated next to
him, a thin white-haired man in a priest's sputane. "Father
Cenci."

Father Cenci held up a frail, veined hand as greeting,
then sat back. I hadn't expected to find another guest in the
car and was slightly put out to have to sit so close to religion. I couldn't remember ever having seen a member of
any faith in San Angelo's company. Even in the hospital,
when it had looked as if he might succumb to the heart
attack that had felled him, he had waved the priest away.
At the time I thought he was frightened by the sudden
presence of the father, a possible manifestation that death
was closer than he wanted to believe. Nor had San Angelo,
in all the years I had known him, ever led me to suspect that
he was in any way a practicing Catholic.

I couldn't help glancing at him from time to time as we
crossed the Triborough Bridge and got onto the throughway
to Connecticut. He looked older than when I had seen him
last. The bags under his eyes were more prominent and
grayer, and his lids were red with tiredness. Of course he'd

been overdoing things for years, working at a tempo which would have left younger men breathless, meetings here, meetings there, mostly up late at nights, drinking heavily and eating with utter disregard for what was good for him. He never took long vacations. His only real recreation were the long weekends in Ridgefield. I reached for the blanket, folded over the back of one of the front seats, and he let me spread it over his knees without pushing it away. That worried me. After a little while he fell asleep, something he did frequently, and I listened to his breathing. It came steadily, evenly. I sighed, relieved. Yet this drive was different from the others. Melinda, who usually chattered incessantly, never opened her eyes to turn around and talk, or to beg us to stop for a brown cow. Mrs. Riley didn't quarrel with her husband about the way he drove; Riley didn't ask for permission to turn on the radio to listen to a game. Tiger didn't stir once but lay like a stuffed animal at my feet. Perhaps, I thought, it was Father Cenci's presence which cast a spell of reverent silence over all of us.

But when we turned from the Pike onto route seven, everything changed. Tiger sat up and barked with excitement, Mrs. Riley's thin, sharp voice could be heard berating Riley for having passed another car too fast, San Angelo woke up and knotted his tie which he had loosened before falling asleep. Father Cenci spoke for the first time since I had been introduced. "Are we there?" And Melinda, trying to yawn and speak at the same time, turned toward us and said, "In about ten minutes. Hi, Tad, when did you get in?"

"At four o'clock."

"I couldn't have been asleep all that time!"

Her face was extraordinarily beautiful, sweet, serene, an old-fashioned face. Her skin was perfectly smooth, without the slightest blemish; one wanted to touch it to see if it was real. Her eyes, a rare deep blue, were set wide apart over a short, haughty nose. Her lips were full and already sensu-

ous, her chin heart-shaped. Because her features were so
well formed and she was tall for her twelve years, she was
often taken for quite a few years older which made her
enormously proud and on occasions caused difficulties. "See
what your pill did to me," she told San Angelo. "I missed the
whole ride. I told you I didn't want to take it. I hate all
pills!"

San Angelo didn't answer her directly but addressed me.
"She was so excited, we simply had to calm her down."

"Like the cats," she said contemptuously. "With a Valium.
And not a half, as they get, but a whole one."

"And what was the excitement about?"

"She's going to Italy," said San Angelo.

"To Italy? What for?"

"Her grandmother wants to see her. She hasn't seen her
since she was a baby and feels it's high time she got acquainted with her grandchild."

Though I had quite often helped Melinda to compose a
dutiful monthly letter to this faraway grandmother in
Rome, the old lady had never quite materialized for me, and
I doubt if she had for Melinda. She was just somebody who
lived in Europe, to whom one had to write about school and
friends and what one did and left undone. The idea that
Melinda should visit her had, as far as I knew, never been
discussed. Or rather just once, when San Angelo had shaken
his head in refusal. "If she wants to see Lindy, she can get
on a plane. First class, for all I care. But Lindy is not leaving
the country as long as I have anything to say." And now he
had changed his mind.

"And when is she going?"

"On Monday."

"So soon?" I had planned to take her skiing in Vermont.

"Christmas vacation," said San Angelo. "As good a time as
any other. Father Cenci is going to take her with him."

"Will you miss me, Tad? You will, won't you?"

"Of course I'll miss you."

"That's good." She smiled with pleasure. A moment later

Riley swung the car sharply to the left and through an iron gate which opened to the electronic eye, into the driveway of Laughing Echo.

We rounded a wide stretch of lawn and pulled up in front of a white clapboard house with simple classical lines. Smoke rose into the clear air from four chimneys, and although it wasn't quite dark yet, every room inside was lit. San Angelo hated the dark. Even when he slept, the house in the country or the apartment in town were always alive with lights. Ernesto, the caretaker and gardener, appeared from the kitchen entrance. San Angelo had a knack for using people in more than one capacity.

"The path's been cleared?" he asked Ernesto now, handing him his briefcase.

"I went through them all with the snowplow this morning."

There had been no snow in New York, just a few wet flurries, but here it lay high and white, and Tiger, who had jumped out of the car the moment Ernesto had opened the door, was leaping across its frozen surface oblivious of the fact that at any moment he might break through and get stuck.

"Then let's go for a walk," said San Angelo. "Come on. Who's going to join me?"

Ernesto was one of the few persons who dared to speak up to his master. "No, Signore." He always pretended not to be able to speak English. "It's bitter cold. Almost zero. Look at the thermometer. You'll wait till morning, when the sun is out. There'll be sun, the radio says. A sunny, clear day."

"Get me my heavy coat, Riley," called San Angelo, but Riley had disappeared inside with the luggage, and Mrs. Riley was already busy in the kitchen, unpacking the food she had brought out.

"It certainly is cold." Father Cenci spoke unexpectedly, his breath a white cloud in the air, and he was trembling in the icy temperature.

"Father. I'm sorry. Come in, come in. Let me give you a

drink to warm you up, and show you your room." I watched
him, one arm around the priest's shoulders, opening the
gaily painted, yellow front door. "Linda, where are you?"
She looked at me, then followed the two men into the
house.

A little more than half a mile away, the woods began. The
cleared path ran like a black ribbon between the snow
banked on either side. Pine, beech, and maple threw blue
shadows onto the meadow, visible at this time of the year
when the trees were not in leaf. I could hear Tiger barking,
chasing a rabbit or a fox, maybe even a deer, and the gur-
gling of water under the ice which had formed over the
brook on my left. Though now I had an explanation for
Father Cenci's presence, I was disturbed by the fact that
San Angelo had not discussed Melinda's trip to Italy with
me, not even told me about his decision to send her to her
maternal grandmother for Christmas. True, I had been at
the office only two days this week, but since I knew how he
loved to have the child near him and I had always been
drawn into everything concerning either of them, I couldn't
understand why this time I had been left out. A wave of
resentment rushed through me, and aware of the fact that it
was resentment, I thought how right Susanne had been
when she had berated me for being so closely involved with
San Angelo.

The first stars became visible above me, and suddenly I
felt the cold. I whistled for Tiger, and when he didn't come,
turned toward home, knowing the dog would sooner or later
find his way to the kitchen, warmth, and food.

Shortly before I reached the house, I spotted Tiger, dig-
ging in a pile of snow. He didn't stop when I came closer.
"What is it?" I asked. "What are you pulling there, Tike?" It
was a piece of wood. Then I saw a pair of boots sticking out
at the far end of the pile. For a moment I stood very still,
my heart beating fast, thinking about what I had read a few
days ago in the newspaper clippings Mrs. Johnson had got

for me. Of the murdered Justice, whose body a dog had discovered under a pile of snow. I knelt down and pushed the snow away with both hands as fast as I could. It was Melinda.

She sat up, laughing, jubilant. "I scared you, didn't I? I really scared you, Tad. Don't deny it."

"What's the big idea?"

"You left me. You didn't ask me to come for a walk with you. I was so sad. Sad and mad. I decided to build a snowman. I haven't built a snowman this year, and I was almost through when I thought how I wouldn't be seeing you for an endless time. And that made me so sad all over again, I wanted to die. So I just lay down and kicked the snowman and all the snow fell on top of me."

"You are even more stupid than I thought," I said sternly. "And you wouldn't have died. You know that as well as I do. But you can catch pneumonia from lying on the frozen ground, and with all that snow on top of you."

"Then I couldn't go to Italy with that old crow. What a pity you found me."

"Get up." I yanked her to her feet. "And look at your hair. It's sopping wet."

"Of course. Snow is water."

"Get into the house and into a hot tub and to bed with you."

"I'll do nothing of the sort," she said. "Stop showing off. You can't order me around like that."

"Then I'll tell your grandfather that unless he wants you to come down with a cold, he'd better make you stay in bed."

"You're not being very nice," she said. "Anyway, it's all your fault. If you hadn't gone off without me . . . I was so miserable. Honestly, I wanted to die."

"Into the house," I said, "a hot bath, hot tea and to bed. Scram now, on the double."

She knew when I meant it and ran into the house,

through the kitchen, offended and furious. I went in by the
main entrance, hung my coat in the hall closet and entered
the living room. Next to the roaring fire sat San Angelo and
Father Cenci. They stopped talking when they noticed me.
A moment of silence, as if I had interrupted an intimate
conversation which they didn't want to share with me, then
San Angelo pointed to the table next to him. "Here, have
some hot tea with rum. You look frozen." He lifted the pot.
"I hope it's still hot."

It wasn't, but before he could ring, I took it from him and
went out into the kitchen to ask Mrs. Riley to boil some
water. I also asked her to be good enough to bring some tea
up to Melinda. "Where's Doug?" Earlier, in the car, I'd
wondered about his absence. "Why isn't he around?"

"It wasn't convenient." She took the boiling water from
the stove and when she had gone, I decided not to join the
men again but sat down at the big kitchen table.

The years fell away. San Angelo had bought Laughing
Echo shortly after my parents died. There he was, a wid-
ower, with two young boys, his son Justo and me. He had
felt strongly that we boys should have a place to roam
around in, or perhaps he had used it as a justification to buy
the property, for he was quite miserly and never spent large
amounts for his own pleasure. This big kitchen with its dining nook had been Justo's and my favorite place. We'd
breakfasted here, and what a breakfast! Country sausages,
fresh eggs, pancakes flooded with cherry syrup, fruit. Never
in time for lunch, we'd sneak a bite from the icebox, and still
hungry after a big supper, would tiptoe down the stairs to
feast on anything we could find. No worries except the usual
ones at that age—would the ice on the little lake down the
meadow be thick enough to skate on? When would we at
last be allowed to use the rifle? Had anybody noticed that
we'd stolen the spare tire? Or the first strawberries? Or
maybe even a few dimes from Mrs. Riley's blue milkpot on
the third shelf, left corner? We didn't bring along many

friends; we didn't need them. We were sufficient unto ourselves. Until Justo met Clarissa.

That summer, with a tutor and four other boys, we'd been shipped off to Europe for half our vacation, and been bored to death by unaccustomed food and museums. But then we had met Clarissa and fallen violently in love with her. Both of us. But she chose Justo, which, with the irrationality of my sixteen years, had caused me anguish. I told her so later, two years after Melinda was born. I could still see her cooking spaghetti for San Angelo, a dish Mrs. Riley never made to his satisfaction. Generously she ignored the fact that at the time I'd been too green to even be considered. "Why Tad," she said, lifting the spaghetti from the colander and into a bowl of egg yolks. "I had no idea. And you never wrote. There was hardly a day when I didn't get a letter from Justo."

As far as I could tell, his writing her so assiduously was the only thing he'd ever kept secret from me. "But for heaven's sake, Clari, didn't you know?"

"No, I didn't." She had smiled, all the time stirring in the crisp, cut-up bacon. "You know, one is never quite sure how you feel. Everybody at table? Then carry this in for me." Dead now. Clarissa and Justo. And it had taken San Angelo and me weeks before we had been able to face Laughing Echo again.

I rinsed my cup, so as to stay in Mrs. Riley's good graces, and went back to the living room. Father Cenci was just pocketing something I couldn't see, and the hi-fi was playing rock 'n' roll. "That record I'd like," he said, moving his thin body to the rhythm of the music.

"You can have them all," San Angelo told him. "Or are there any you'd like to keep, Tad?"

"No," I said. "But Lindy might want to have first choice."

San Angelo said nothing, and Father Cenci continued to sway, quite gracefully too. I looked at him, surprised, and he stopped. "I want them for my church," he explained, "or

the young won't come, not unless I can offer them something."

I hadn't thought of him as that modern, but he laughed.
"The little children and the old people wouldn't fill half the
pews. And I like to keep my eye on the teen-agers. Like
everybody else I'm having trouble with them."

"Drugs?"

"A lot of grass and hash, thank God very little of the hard
stuff, but alcohol is just as much of a problem. Cheap mus-
catel, mostly. Some hard liquor. And of course, beer. Too
little food, so it hits them quickly. A lot of pregnancies at
much too young an age. I'm grateful for the pill, but the
mothers are against it. They're torn between what to regard
as the greater sin—sleeping out of wedlock or what, for
them, is murder."

Drinks and hot appetizers. Then Mrs. Riley came in. "Mr.
San, Lindy doesn't feel well. She'd like to stay in bed."

I had to smile. For once she was obeying.

San Angelo got up. "Is she running a temperature? Maybe
we should have stayed in town. I'd better have a look at
her."

After he had closed the door, Father Cenci turned to me.
"If he's not the most generous man"—he patted the pocket
under his soutane—"and I never even have to mention the
sad state of my parish. But this is the biggest sum I've ever
received."

"How long have you known him?"

My question seemed to surprise him. "Why, all his life,"
he said. "I was present at his birth. And all through his
childhood and youth. I remember him pushing the cart
when his mother was too pregnant to work. He was so small,
he could hardly move the heavy thing, or let the brakes
down when a customer wanted to rummage in what he had
to offer. His father was a junk dealer, as you know."

So it was true, the story I had taken with a grain of salt
and which San Angelo liked to tell as if he derived deep

satisfaction from this example of the opportunities his adopted country offered to the poorest immigrant.

"And it was your father who opened up another world to him."

"Yes." I knew, I'd been told many times how my father had started San on the schooling that was to lead, in the end, to a partnership in my father's firm. But I didn't mind hearing it again from Father Cenci. It was a romantic story, unreal in today's light.

"He was a cab driver. Your father and he got to talking the first time San picked him up. After that he made it his business to be in front of your parents' house in the morning, at the time your old man used to leave, and outside the office building in the afternoon to take him home. For some reason, the law fascinated San. Perhaps because he'd seen too much of how it could be bent and too many lawyers who made fortunes helping people to evade it. So he went to night school. When your father saw how impatient he was to get things done, he gave San the money to study full time. In two years he had his degree, another two and he'd paid your father back. Oh, he was ambitious, but ambitious in an honest direction. A rarity, and unique in his neck of the woods. And he was wild. There were times when I was afraid he'd end up in a reformatory or jail. He had no control over his emotions, no one dared cross him, except his mother. She was a formidable woman, afraid of nothing. She'd quietly fill a pot with cold water and empty it over him if he fought his Papa, or his brothers, or anyone for that matter. One day she grabbed the nearest pot handy, but it was boiling water. San was in the hospital for weeks. Bellevue was a lesson to him. He learned to control himself. I often marvel at how calm and wise he has become."

I didn't want to tell the father that San Angelo had never mentioned him to me. I didn't want to hurt his feelings. But I managed to ask him in a roundabout way why, since San Angelo was obviously not religious, he had kept up a relationship with him. "He has strayed from the church," said Father Cenci, with a sweet, gentle smile, "but he will come back. Meanwhile he lives in faith. He comes to confession."

And there you think you know a man you see every day, in whose house you have grown up, whose work and play you have shared. I would never have dreamed that San Angelo ever went to confession.

Father Cenci pushed the platter with the appetizers over to me. "Tad . . . if I may call you that . . . he's worried about you."

"Worried about me?"

"He says you're a hothead, worse than he was at your age. That you speak too openly with people you don't know well. That one day you'll find yourself in trouble. I understand you've already been clubbed over the head and arrested in some demonstration or other. He wonders if he did the right thing when he recommended you to the commission. You may have to deal with the Administration, and be too outspoken . . ."

"He means politically. We don't agree on many political issues, granted, but my God, we're not living under a dictatorship yet!"

San Angelo came back. "No temperature," he said. "I think she's just sulking and wants to let us know, by not appearing for dinner, how much she resents being sent away."

We went into the dining room with its old paneled walls and crossbeams and ate a leisurely meal, rinsing down the good food with three bottles of red wine. But I was annoyed over San Angelo's criticism, voiced to a stranger, and stuck stubbornly to the subject of the disastrous state of our domestic affairs. Finally San Angelo shoved the peppermill over to me, making enough noise with it to stop my tirade. "Look here, Tad, you're talking like a foreigner who reads nothing but the sensational tabloids. No single man is going to ruin this country. It's too strong, too healthy not to pull itself together when things get bad enough. That's when sanity always manifests itself." Again he looked very tired, and I decided to leave him his illusions. Later San Angelo and the father sat down to play chess. I watched for a while, then took Tiger out. A full moon hung above the woods, but it was too cold, and I went upstairs to the room I had been given when I was eight years old, a corner room which looked out across the swimming pool and the small lake to the north, and faced the driveway to the east. The little pile of snow under which Melinda had buried herself was still there.

CHAPTER

SIX

I HAD JUST PULLED the comforter over me when there was
a soft knock on my door. Without waiting for me to
answer, Melinda came in. "Am I disturbing you?"

She was wearing one of those short outfits girls her age
were so fond of. A longish tunic over short panties. I threw
her the quilt. "Cover up." She rolled herself in it until she
looked like a patchwork sausage, then lay down on the thick
woolen rug beside my bed. "Isn't it too cold on the floor?"

"I brought my hot water bottle." She showed it to me,
then tucked it back over her stomach. "Did you have a good
dinner? What did you eat?"

"A saddle of deer."

"With red cabbage and lingonberries and apple sauce."

"That's right."

"All I got was the apple sauce." She made a face. "A light
meal. A cup of soup, vegetables out of a can, and apple
sauce. Did you order that for me?"

"No."

I glanced at the book I'd brought out and she caught my
eyes wandering. "I know you want to read, but really, Tad,
I'll be gone in a few days."

I put the book down. "Why don't you want to go? You

should be thrilled and looking forward to it. Think of walking streets you've never seen."

"There are plenty of streets in America I've never seen."

"But cobblestone streets."

"They're hell on your feet. Look at Ernesto's. He has bunions as big as pullet eggs from walking on them for so many years. Anyway, I've seen it all on television."

"For God's sake . . . Europe on television. You can't mean it."

She said nothing.

"And you'll meet your grandmother."

"Undoubtedly old and fat. I don't like old women. I don't ever want to be an old woman. I'm going to die young, while I'm still pretty."

"Look darling, you seem to have made up your mind to hate everything and everybody before you've even been there. Try to look forward to it. You're going to fly for the first time."

"And what if the plane crashes? Have you thought of that?"

"No. And I won't. Or are you afraid of flying?"

"I'm not afraid of anything."

"At times I wish you were."

"Oh, stop being a bore, Tad. Don't lecture me, please. I'm unhappy enough."

I patted her head and she looked up. Her eyes were filled with tears. At once I melted. "What is it darling? Why are you so unhappy?"

"I'm thinking of all of you having fun, putting up the Christmas tree. Last time I picked one out with Ernesto, and now I won't even see it."

"Without you there'll be no tree."

"Great help! And what about my presents?"

"I'll have them all lined up for you when you get back."

"And the skiing trip you promised me? And having to think of you swishing around with Susy?"

Yes, Melinda and Susy had met, and disliked each other instantly. I had tried to bring them together again because I felt strongly that Melinda needed a woman for a friend, with whom she might talk differently than to San Angelo and me, or to the girls in school. But Susy had said, "That precocious brat? Really, Tad, I have better things to do with my free time." And Melinda had shrugged when I had asked her how she liked Susy. "I don't like people who behave as if they owned a person. It's true. She treats you as if you were her property, and no right of way for anybody else."

"I won't be swishing around with Susy," I said, and didn't know why I told her. It just happened. "We're not seeing each other any longer."

"Cool," she said. "Doug and I broke up too." So that was why he hadn't been invited. "He's too jealous. Too possessive. But of course we always make up again. That's part of the fun of breaking up." She lifted her head and looked me in the eye with a strange intensity. "With you and Susy . . . is it just for the time being or did you really call it quits?"

"I'm afraid so."

"Did she tell you to go or did you?"

"It was mutual."

I had meant to talk to San Angelo about it on the ride out, but there hadn't been an opportunity. "San will be happy," said Melinda, as if she could read my thoughts.

I lit a cigarette. "Why do you say that?"

"Because I think so."

I couldn't very well question her, but it didn't seem likely that San Angelo had ever discussed my girlfriend with her. Whenever I had spoken to him about Susy, he had been noncommittal, and I hadn't mentioned her often because she conjured up the memory of that dreadful day.

"Tad," said Melinda, in a curiously flat voice but with eyes as big as saucers. "Will you marry me?"

Just as when Susanne had asked, I was taken by surprise. "Marry you? Why, Lindy—I've never given it a thought. You're my little sister, a little girl."

"In four years I won't be a little girl, and I'll be very beautiful."

"You may be."

"And I'm a woman already, if you know what I mean."

Three weeks ago she had started to menstruate. San Angelo had shown me the medical report of her checkup. "You've not answered me," she said.

"Well, it's very flattering. But why do you want to marry me?"

"You're just right for me. A lot of fun when you come off your high horse, and nice. And it would make San very happy. He's leaving all he has to us, in equal parts. You know how he is—it would all stay in the family."

"You should never marry a man for pragmatic reasons."

"What's 'pragmatic'?"

"Practical. Like San."

"Four years aren't too long, Tad. That's what you always say when I want something for which I'm supposed to be too young. Time flies. It'll fly for us."

I thought of Susy and how I had told her she was out of her mind to think that San Angelo was planning for me to marry his granddaughter.

"And what am I supposed to do in those four years?"

"Oh, you could sleep around, with girls that are just good in bed. But not afterward."

I stared at her. I almost asked: What do you know about girls that are "just good in bed"? But she was smiling sweetly, innocently.

"Lindy," I said. "I think we'd better discuss this four years from now. If I'm still free and you still feel the same way about me . . ."

She reached up suddenly and with one quick, sure gesture turned out the light beside my bed. Darkness filled the room. "What is it?"

"Sh!"

Steps could be heard on the staircase. San Angelo and Father Cenci were coming up. "Why did you turn out the light?" There had been plenty of times when she had come to my room for a chat before going to bed, or I had gone to hers for a good-night talk. But she didn't answer. A door opened and closed, then another.

"I'd better go," said Melinda. "San might want to say good night. He usually does." I could hear her running across the floor, then she came back and threw the eiderdown on my bed. "I almost took it along. You won't promise anything?"

"No," I said. "Definitely not."

"But it would be so comforting to know."

"Good night, darling. Let's wait four years. How did it go? Times flies. Sleep tight."

She threw me a kiss. Not that I could see her; I only heard her kissing her hand, then snapping her fingers. "I think I could love you very much."

It took me a long time to fall asleep. I was strangely moved by the whole thing. Melinda was a jigsaw puzzle of contrast—her childishness, her sophistication, her games of make believe, her sense of reality, defiant yet pliable, courageous yet afraid, her absolute naturalness and her airs, all so clearly and pathetically transparent. Feeling lost when she should have felt safe and safe when she should have been cautious. Why had she touched me when Susanne had not? I tried to picture her in my mind, grown-up. Indeed, as she had just told me with such assurance, she would be very beautiful. And her spirit, her zest for living, which had been absent tonight, would be overpowering. I smiled as I recalled her condition—I might amuse myself during the four years of waiting, but not after we were married. For a girl who hated anyone possessive? But what I was really puzzling over was the question—had the idea of a future marriage been hers, or had San Angelo planted the seed of such a possibility in her mind?

I reached for Robert Winslow's Cross-National Study, which Dermot had suggested I read, but found it hard to concentrate on the endless charts and statistics.

CHAPTER

SEVEN

I N THE AFTERNOON of the last day of the year, Dermot
phoned. He had finally managed to round up some
of the men who had been chosen to give their opinions
on The Effect of Violence on the Judiciary and Terror as a
Measure of Influencing Judicial Decisions. By chance all of
them happened to be in town. Would I come to the third
floor, please, to meet them?

The office I entered could be in no way compared to the
shabby little room I had been given. Here the walls were
paneled with dark brown, aged oak. The light fell from little
holes in the ceiling, large windows looked out on Foley
Square, the shades were neither dirty nor torn. A large
table, covered with green baize, comfortable chairs, upholstered in genuine green leather. Glasses of water, pads and
sharpened pencils in various colors in front of each seat.
There were only seven people. A Senator, who was the
chairman of the commission, surprisingly old and looking
his age, moving in a dignified fashion and slightly somno-
lent; a Congressman from a New England state, newly
elected; a psychiatrist from Rochester, middle-aged and
permanently smiling, more to himself than at any of us; a
judge from Maine, looking like a Grant Wood portrait come

to life; a minister from Vermont, in his dark somber cloth; a historian from Harvard University; and Dermot. They were seated at the table like jewels on exhibit for their specific value, and I was surprised when they rose to shake hands with me. Different as they were in appearance and attitude, they all seemed somehow related by the awareness of their eminence, and linked to each other by an arrogance which didn't manifest itself in any particular manner but was there just the same, like a smog clouding their humanity.

After Dermot had introduced me, the Senator made a little speech which he had undoubtedly made often with only slight changes. It was insignificant, and the only good thing about it was that it was short. He pointed out some of the areas the Kerner Commission had identified in its report— the overcrowding of jails, the breakdown of evidence, the dispensing of multi- rather than individual justice, the setting of high, unindividualized bail. Then he pointed out the obvious peril—that the government might see itself forced to take special action against specific groups, riots, demonstrations, to prevent guerrilla warfare. The historian went back to the whole bloody period of the French Revolution, worked his way up to Sacco and Vanzetti, and the opinion held by many that they had been executed as a response to public hysteria; to the vigilantes' activities in the West, and ended up with the Watts riots where, within two days, four thousand people had been jailed and it had been impossible to give any kind of trial. As he spoke, he kept breaking matches into tiny pieces. I watched, fascinated, as the pile in front of him grew and grew, and when he swept it from the table, I could imagine the floor of his study littered with broken matches until, crushed by the heavy weight of his body stepping on them, they turned to sawdust. I decided he must have recently given up smoking and had to keep his hands busy. All through the world, he said, in every century, people had rebelled against laws that seemed unjust or stood in the way of their endeavors. But laws, even if unpopular, were necessary if an administration was to function. Even if it meant, he added, with an attempt at humor, that each Justice would have to be given a bodyguard. The judge from Maine shook his head. Force created counterforce, and counterforce, possibly, revolution.

They said the things usually said on occasions such as this, when there was no audience to inspire nor the press to quote them, handicapped to some extent by the fear that their pearls of wisdom might be stolen by someone present, to be worn eventually as his own, and trying desperately not to show off. Yet each one of them gave you the feeling that, if he so chose, he could display the power behind his fame in an eloquent and scholarly opinion. The Congressman brought the Newark riots back to memory, the courts that hadn't been able to handle the situation, the bail system that no longer worked, the fact that lawyers were prevented from seeing their clients. "Who says it can't happen here? In other countries republics or democracies have turned into dictatorships." And after a few more words on the grave dangers facing every free nation today, he turned to the psychiatrist and asked him whom he would recommend for a member of his family who had suddenly displayed suicidal tendencies. The minister from Vermont wanted to know with whom to get in touch in Europe or Asia, without having to take too much time from his parish and incur too great expenses, and Dermot tinkled his glass and told them that this was where I came in. I would do my best to ease their load and contact whatever famous counterparts in foreign countries they might want to reach, sparing them telephone calls and correspondence, and introducing them, however well known they might be, to strangers, equally well known, and just as anxious not to waste any time. They could call on me if they needed anything or wanted some special service attended to. Suddenly everybody was smiling benevolently at me, and getting up, making excuses for their hurry, but after all, this was New Year's Eve. One man had brought his wife along for the celebrations, someone else had to catch a plane if he didn't want to miss the party at home, another wanted to see a show for which he had bought tickets months in advance. They were human after all, human in their delight to have found someone else to do the footwork for them. I began to feel like the boy in school to whom a mean teacher has given the chore of cleaning the blackboard, seeing that the chalk is in place, collecting the class papers and carrying them down an endless passage to his room.

Perhaps, if it hadn't been for the Christmas holidays, curiously void of festivity with Melinda away, if Susanne hadn't gone out of my life and my volunteer work on the Lower Eastside been more urgently needed, I might not have pursued a question that had bothered me, as well as thousands of other people, ever since Justice Butworth's body had been discovered. Why, after more than three weeks, wasn't there the slightest trace of the murderer? I was aware of course that some crimes were never solved, that others took endless time to bring to a conclusion, and in this case the circumstances had been extraordinarily auspicious for an assassination. A dark, snowy night, an hour when nobody in his right mind would venture into Central Park alone. No witnesses. But who had known that the Justice would be in New York on this specific weekend? In that neighborhood? And why had he gone into the park? To meet someone? Or had he been followed ever since he had left his home in Washington, taken a plane, reached New York and finally the place where he had been killed? Who had planned his murder? What group of men were responsible?

"The whole case is unusual," San Angelo said. "For most people the Court is a concept rather than something with which they can identify. It's too symbolic for that. The members are not elected, they rarely come into physical contact with the people since they don't campaign, nor are they given time on television. They're not flesh and blood, and to single out one of them . . ." He scratched his head.

"But that isn't altogether true anymore," I said. "Ever since the Kennedy assassination and the Warren Report, the judges have come into much sharper focus as human beings. People have grown to look upon them as lawmakers, and identify them with certain laws with which they may or may not agree and therefore hold a Justice personally responsible. Social reactions are stronger than ever. Besides, San, the Court was never as immune as you like to think. During the last hundred and fifty years, several judges have been killed. And if you take them one by one . . . most of them because of personal grudges. Crawford, for instance, by a man he had sentenced to life imprisonment. And look at Field and Terry. And Slough was shot because he refused to retract some insulting remarks he had made. Naturally there were also bigger issues . . ."

"I know all that." San Angelo sounded weary. "But it's beyond my imagination that someone should have murdered Butworth for personal reasons. You're on the wrong track, Tad. Don't go off on tangents. Try to remember that your job is the effect of violence on the courts, *not* the violence itself."

I don't know why this conversation only served to strengthen my feelings that there was a different motive behind the Butworth assassination than the one generally assumed, but it did.

"You'll get nine-one-one right away," Mrs. Johnson told me when I tried to call police, "but to get anybody at Manhattan North to answer might take longer."

As usual, her information turned out to be correct. Almost forty minutes went by until I was told that Lieutenant Jenkins of homicide was not in. He didn't work every day. "That's a job I'd like to have."

"I doubt it, sir," said a young voice, and I could hear the receiver being slammed down. I couldn't face trying again for a connection, but wrote a letter explaining who I was and that I was authorized to request any help in the fulfillment of my job. I left a message for Lieutenant Jenkins to call me at his earliest convenience. He didn't find it convenient to call me during the next three days. I was too impatient to wait any longer. Mrs. Johnson called the police commissioner for me. He told her he'd see me any time.

I walked up Centre Street and over to his office. You can never tell how things will go once they get into official hands. This time they went quickly, efficiently, no waste motion. He listened to what I had to say, nodded, told his secretary to get Lieutenant Jenkins at homicide, Twenty-fourth Precinct, on the phone, talked to him, hand in front of mouth, and said, "You can go over now if you want to. A hundred and fifty-one West One Hundred. Fourth floor."

There was a parking lot on the corner where I was lucky enough to find a place. An old man was selling chestnuts. I bought a bag. I never could resist them. I walked past a small church with a gothic spire and a New York Bloomingdale Public Library Branch, then crossed over to the precinct building. It was flanked on one side by a playground, on the other by Ladder 22, Eleventh Battalion, Engine Company 76. Two firetrucks were just moving out.

Most police stations are dismal old buildings, wrought-iron fencing around them, garbage spilling over, firetraps, but this one was an exception. It stood among high apartment buildings, clean, air-conditioned, modern. A black policeman was leaning against one of the glass doors, almost blocking a sign that read, PISTOL RANGE IN THE BASEMENT. I walked past him into the lobby. To my right was a waiting room—tables, wooden armchairs, cigarette machine, Coca-Cola dispenser. Quite a few people—a poor old woman with crutches, a baby crying, a boy cursing loudly in Spanish. To my left, behind a counter, the usual black wall, the recharging board for walkie-talkies. There also was a desk with a cop who tried to stop me, then pointed to another desk from which a black lady was smiling at me. As soon as she heard my name, she waved me on. "This way, sir." Obviously she had been given orders.

Fourth floor. A small office. A tall, blondish man looked up from behind his desk. Regulation height, I thought, five feet eight, and his eyes must have been twenty-twenty. He didn't rise, just pointed to a chair. He was smoking a pipe which instantly made him sympathetic to me.

"Bad timing," he said. "We had a crew from some television station with us for almost two weeks and no homicide. Then, yesterday, just after they pulled out, three in a row. And now there might be a lull again. You never know."

"I'm afraid you've got me wrong. The commissioner phoned. I'm Wood. Thaddeus J. Wood." I pulled out my identification and shoved it across the desk to him. "Glad you could see me."

Jenkins wasted no time. "What do you want? I don't know if I can be of any help."

"Anything new on Butworth?"

"On Justice Butworth?"

"Yes. Are you any closer to solving the case?"

"Solving it?" He grinned. "Don't you know, Wood, that at best twenty percent of all crimes are solved? We don't even have a trace. Sure, some crank calls, letters accusing this or that person, this or that organization, but nothing's come of any of them, and believe me, we're thorough. If we find the killer it will be accidentally, if you ask me."

I peeled another chestnut. "It always puzzled me that he wasn't recognized immediately. He was only identified at the morgue. Correct?"

"And then only by chance. Of course we'd have found out eventually by fingerprints. The guy who put him in the freezer was rough. He pushed the drawer shut before Butworth was quite in, and his wig got caught on the rim of the drawer. That's when the medical examiner was called back."

"You mean a toupee?"

"Not if you're thinking of those things people use to hide a bald spot or give the impression they still have a lot of hair. No. This was a real wig. It changed his whole physiognomy. Made in France, it said, with an address on the Faubourg St. Honoré. He was wearing a beard too, not a bushy one, a neat, pointed little Vandyke, and a mustache that went nicely with it. The whole bit gave a completely different shape to his cheeks, chin, and mouth, sort of elongating them, except the mouth. That looked fuller and squarer than it actually was. Of course then all hell broke loose. Instead of the next day, the autopsy was done at once. The fingerprints that had been taken in Central Park were immediately checked in Albany and Washington, and everybody was notified. I was present when the corpse was searched, and I still can't understand why the wig didn't come off when they put the body in the bag. Or later, when they unzipped it and took it out."

"The papers never mentioned it."

"No. That was withheld." He seemed to glance at my identification which was still lying on his desk, or maybe I just imagined it. "There were photos taken?"

"Of course. First where we found him, then at the morgue."

"Could I see them? Particularly the ones with the wig and beard, and those without."

"The FBI has them." He relit his pipe, and for a while I didn't speak. Then I asked him if he thought Butworth could possibly have been murdered for personal motives.

"I couldn't say. Anything's possible these days. My instinct has so often been proved wrong; I no longer dare rely on it. As for hunches . . ."

"Psychics have hunches," I said.

"And there are some excellent mediums," said Jenkins. "I remember a case. A woman killed by strangulation. Circumstances pointed to her husband, but he swore he hadn't done it. We had him in several times but couldn't crack the case.

Still all of us were convinced that he'd killed the woman. He agreed to come to a séance. Evidently he didn't think much of it. And there we were, in semidarkness, and as soon as the spirit entered the medium, she pointed at the man and spoke in the voice of the dead woman, or so it must have seemed to him. Anyway, he drowned himself a couple of hours later."

"Then why not try a medium or a psychic on Butworth's case?"

He shook his head. "We thought about it but then decided against it."

"Why?"

But Jenkins just shrugged without giving me a reason.

The silence between us became awkward. Finally I broke it. "Is there anything else you could tell me that might be of interest to me?"

He looked at me hard and long. "Trying to take my job away from me? Because what I've just told you isn't exactly relevant to your function on the commission, is it?"

I had been afraid he would eventually reach this conclusion and had to find an explanation. It came without too much effort. "I'm going to see Miss Butworth next week, and I wondered how much she'd been told, so I wouldn't say the wrong thing."

It wasn't a very good justification for my visit, but Jenkins chose to accept it. "She knows about the wig and the beard," he said, "but we don't want it to go any further."

CHAPTER

EIGHT

MAYBE I'D INTENDED ALL ALONG, subconsciously, to talk to Miss Butworth, but having mentioned it to Jenkins, the vague intention assumed reality. Just as something you feel becomes a fact you can no longer escape when you write it down. I begged off an extra day from San Angelo, who nodded, too busy with a contract to ask questions. I took a plane to Washington. Many people like the capital. I don't. To me it seems as disorganized as its momentary handling of the country. Full of promises that remain unfulfilled, and blatantly pretentious, even its beautiful and majestic spots like the hopes of people who want to trust their government, but beauty alone can't solve the thousand problems that beset the nation.

I took a taxi to Georgetown and the address given in the newspapers, where Miss Butworth had gone to stay with her mother. A maid in proper old-fashioned attire—dull, black, alpaca dress, white lacy apron—opened the door on the third ring. "Mrs. Butworth is not in."

"I know. Would you please ask Miss Butworth if she would see me?" I handed her my card, also my identification. She didn't even look at them. "Miss Butworth isn't here."

"You mean she doesn't want to see anyone. I can understand that. But if you would just let me in, maybe . . ." I tried to slip her a ten dollar bill.

"Oh no, sir," she said, with great dignity, and closed the door. I went around the block, came back and rang again. This time she didn't come to the door but called from a basement window, "I told you she wasn't here. Please stop bothering us." Then suddenly something seemed to change her mind. "She's gone back to New York."

I had some time to kill between planes, so I went to see George Kollam, one of the most eminent criminologists in the country, whom I had asked to write a paper on terror as a reaction to unpopular laws. He was just leaving his house when I waylaid him on his doorstep and walked with him until he found a taxi. "Yes, yes," he said. "But I doubt if it's going to do much good."

"It's great. Didn't you get my wire of congratulation?"

"It's above everybody's head," he replied with an arrogance that left me speechless. I thought I had understood it all right. "Now, if you're going to have it edited, if he changes a word, I'll withdraw my opinion altogether."

I had run into this kind of attitude before and had the usual answer ready. "Of course you'll see it before it goes to press. I'll get the galleys to you as soon as they're ready. Don't pay any attention to what may have been changed or left out, just put back what you want."

"You don't understand," he said irritably. "I don't have time for that sort of thing. Nothing's to be changed, and I expect you to see to that. I know you people. You bend meanings to suit yourselves. You do it all the time." He climbed into the cab, still vexed, but he had a point. I decided to take it up with the editor, not a task I was looking forward to.

I was back in New York by four. Already at La Guardia, I looked up Miss Butworth in the telephone book. There were only three people with that name, two were men, one, a woman, Caroline Butworth. Nineteenth Street. One hundred and forty-nine East Nineteenth Street.

It was a long walk to my car, almost twenty minutes. My bad luck continued—traffic was heavier than I'd anticipated; instead of the usual thirty-five minutes, it took me over an hour to get downtown. After I'd parked near Broadway, I called Mrs. Johnson. Bless the woman. She was still in the office. "Caroline Butworth," I told her. "She lives in New York."

"I know she does."

Her answer made me feel like an ass. "Do you also happen to know what she does? I mean, does she have a profession?"

"Some write-up said she was a photographer."

Why hadn't I read this piece of information, or if I had, why had I forgotten it? "Thanks," I said. "See you tomorrow. And have a drink on me tonight." She liked Manhattans.

The house was only three stories high, a narrow brownstone. I pressed the bell alongside her name, not her full name though, just Caroline. It didn't give the floor she lived on, nor did the door open. Instead a voice through the speaker asked who it was.

"Wood," I said. "Thaddeus Wood. We have an appointment."

"Impossible. I never make appointments after five."

"But my secretary said she'd arranged it with yours. It's the only time I could come. After office hours."

A slight pause, then, "There's nothing in my book."

"Maybe she forgot to put it down." Again a slight pause. I tried to sound more sure. "It must have slipped her mind."

"Wood," she repeated. "That's what you said, isn't it?" She seemed to be wavering, then, reverting to her former severity, said, "Impossible. Besides, my big light isn't working."

"I'm an excellent electrician."

"It's not just the fuse or the bulb. I think it's the wiring."

"My specialty."

"Third floor. Three A."

There was no elevator, and I ran up three rather steep staircases with small landings between. On each one I had to stop and rest, like an old man. Obviously I wasn't in good form. Too much smoking, too much drinking, and too little exercise. With Melinda in Italy, I hadn't gone skiing either. On the third floor, in front of Miss Butworth's door, I vowed to myself that all this would change.

Her door stood ajar, but when I pushed against it, a chair prevented me from entering. Her face showed up in the semidark. There was too little light from the hallway to see her clearly, but she took her time sizing me up before she unfastened the chain and said, "Come in." She didn't bother to shake hands but walked straight ahead of me into a rather small living room. A love seat and a round, marble-topped dining table with four modern Italian chairs around it, black polished ebony frames with acrylon straw seats. On the table stood a bottle of Aquavit, some olives, and on a wooden platter, a large, very German sausage.

"I was having a drink. Care for one?"

She reached for another glass from a nearby shelf. "I've only got Aquavit."

"That's fine with me."

She had the kind of mouth you wanted to make curve into a smile, a large, generous mouth that drooped a little at the corners. One day there would be sharp lines that even the most skilled surgeon wouldn't be able to fix. She wore no makeup, and I wondered what she would look like with some mascara on her eyes and her lashes blackened. They were long, casting little half moons on her high cheekbones, incredibly long, incredibly colorless, but real. Her short hair was a strange shade, like an autumn leaf, almost yellow, with little red lights in it. It clung to her head like a blond Astrakhan cap, short and curly. Her nose was small, slightly upturned, and stuffed up. "I'm sorry," she said, "I have a cold. But I don't think I'm contagious anymore."

I lifted my glass. "Cheerio."

She let me drink it all, never saying a damn word, just sitting there, watching me. When I had finished, she pointed with her head to a half-open sliding door behind her. "The light's in the studio, if you want to try."

I hadn't lied. I did know quite a bit about wiring, and with the tools from the emergency kit she brought from the kitchen, I managed to fix the spotlight. "But you should have it looked at properly."

"I will."

She was leaning against the wall. She was quite small, with surprisingly long legs, wearing jeans, a heavy sweater that looked hand knitted, and no shoes. Her feet were the most beautiful thing about her, long and thin, with each toe perfectly formed, like the feet of Renaissance women.

"Are you really in such a hurry to have your picture taken?"

"Yes. For a birthday present."

"When is the birthday?"

"Ten days from now."

"I couldn't possibly have them ready in ten days."

"Well, that's disappointing."

"I have work piled up to last me for weeks."

"Couldn't you make an exception?"

"I never do. If I promise a thing, I do it. And I have obligations to the people who came before you." She took a long pole from somewhere, and stretching on tiptoe, began to pull the curtains across the skylight. "I don't really like to work at night, but since you're here . . . Walk around a bit. Sit down. Do you smoke? Then light a cigarette."

There were two blown-up plastic chairs. I almost tipped one over as I tried to pose. "Not that way . . . this way." She sounded slightly impatient as she sat down in the other chair to show me. "They're really quite comfortable."

"I don't think so."

"Get your can in the curve and lean into it."

I tried, but she shook her head. "How do you usually relax?"

"On the floor."

It wasn't true, but it gave me a chance to see her feet better. She left the room to get her camera. A Leica. While she was gone, the studio seemed void of life, but once she came back it was filled with a strange electricity, an almost elemental force, like the sea which, when calm, still is active with the unknown depths of life. She shot rapidly, ordering me around all the time. "Look up, to the left, now to the right. Over your shoulder. What's the matter with your left eye?"

"The optical nerve got hurt in an accident."

"Take your glasses off."

I did, but she shook her head. "You can't be natural, can you? You're so tense. Self-conscious. Too aware that your left profile is better than your right. Can't you forget it for a moment?" She walked around some gadgets and switched on music. I smiled. It was a Rubenstein record. Liszt. "He's got twenty hands when he plays that one."

"But more soul in his Schubert."

She reloaded her camera. Stopped the record. "What's your favorite poem? Can you quote it?"

"I'm a lawyer," I told her. "I could quote you a brief."

"Oh, no," she said, quickly. Then, "Your hair's too long."

"It isn't really," I said, startled by the sudden change in the conversation. I had let it grow a few inches in the back and rather liked the way it curled slightly at the nape of my neck.

"I think it spoils your profile."

Again she shot rapidly, then sighed. "Let's try you on the couch."

The couch seemed to sag when I sat down on it, and when I swung my legs up, it rippled under its fur throw like water. She laughed, but it didn't change the seriousness of her eyes and mouth. "It's a waterbed. And it's heated."

She went over to the table. "It gets damn cold in here sometimes, and it warms me when I need it." She poured another
drink, and brought it over to me. "I want you completely
relaxed."

Stretched out now fully, I could feel the warmth of the
heated water seep through my body. "Where do you get
these things?"

"At Bloomingdale's." She sat down on a stool on the other
side of the room, watching me as I tossed down the Aquavit
and put the glass on the floor. I crossed my arms under my
head and stared up at the shaded skylight. Definitely there
was a draft. The material she had pulled across the panes
was moving as if it were alive, breathing in and out, in and
out. Her eyes were somehow disturbing, yet I felt strangely
at peace. I had, I thought, never really been at peace with
Susanne. Perhaps we'd been too competitive. Not actually a
mature relationship. A game, rather. But it had been fun to
play.

"It's no use," she said. "You just can't seem to let go.
You're still uncomfortable."

Was I? I was. I was also starting to feel uneasy about
having tricked her. "Maybe," I said, "it's because . . . well, I
lied to you. I didn't have an appointment."

"I know," she said, and clicked the camera.

"You do? How?"

"Because, dear Mr. Wood, I don't have a secretary."

The camera clicked again. I wasn't sure if I was visibly
blushing or not, but I'd been taught that if you have to
defend yourself, the best way is to attack. "Then why did
you let me come up?"

She was shooting away, the extended lens aimed at me
like a gun. "You sounded . . . well, sort of desperate."

"Desperate? I don't think I've ever felt desperate."

"Then I envy you."

"Have you?"

"Yes. Often. But we're not talking about me. Maybe I was

mistaken, but it seemed to me that there was an urgency in your voice."

I hadn't been aware of any urgency on my part, but perhaps I was wrong. "And you let anybody come up who sounds desperate?"

"That depends."

"On what?"

"My mood."

She put the camera down and went back to the table. This time she filled her glass without asking me if I wanted another drink. I picked up mine and held it out to her.

"There isn't anymore," she said, without embarrassment or apologizing for drinking what was left when, after all, she was the hostess. "What do you want, Mr. Wood? I can guess, of course. You came to talk about my father's death. That's obvious. Well, I'm not going to." She aimed her camera at me again.

"Let's stop that," I told her and got up from the waterbed. "Why do you go on taking pictures when you know I don't need them?"

"You have an interesting face. A little too conventional, still . . ."

"Have dinner with me. Luchow's isn't far away."

She shook her head.

"If you don't like German food, we could go to Casey's. Anywhere you like."

"I told you, I've got a backlog of work."

"Caroline," I said, "you look awfully tired. Forget about work. Let me take you to dinner somewhere."

Again she shook her head. "I want to use up this roll."

"How many left?"

"Three."

When the film was finished, I tried again. "Get your coat. Come on. I promise not to talk about your father."

She disappeared, I hoped, to get her coat. Again there was that feeling of being abandoned in an empty room with

everything around me stagnant, lifeless. Then I heard her
call. "I've got lots of food in the ice box."

I followed the sound of her voice into the kitchen. It was
astonishingly compact. Icebox, freezer, electric stove, all
arranged in a row. Under two sinks a dishwasher and garbage disposer. "I like good equipment, not only for my
work. That's what I spend my money on. For me it's agony
to work with poor tools. The dishes are in the cupboard to
the left and the cutlery's in the chest underneath. I hope
you don't mind eating in the kitchen. I always do. It saves
time." But I carried everything out into the living room and
set the table there and lit two candles which I found next to
some glasses on a shelf. Maybe I was imposing, but I didn't
want to be disturbed by dripping faucets or the hum of
machinery. She said nothing about my ignoring her wish to
eat in the kitchen, her mouth just drooped a little more and
I almost touched it to move the corners up, but restrained
myself. She had heated some soup with little chunks of meat
and lots of vegetables in it, there was a platter of cold cuts
and a green salad, a choice of cheeses and a basket of fresh,
glossy fruit. And with it all, an icebox-cold bottle of San-
cerre. Susanne and I had eaten like this, by candlelight, but
she didn't share my interest in food and was always impatient
to get the meal over with, bustling around while I was still
enjoying it, eager to have everything cleaned up and put
away. Caroline ate ravenously. "Haven't had anything all
day."

"That's not exactly healthy."

"I know. But I can't work when I'm full."

"I can't either."

Not a very interesting conversation, just little odds and
ends of personal likes and dislikes, yet everything we said
seemed important. I asked her why she had chosen photography as a profession and she told me that she had had no
other talents and no particular enthusiasm for any other
subject. "If I could paint well enough, I might have gone on

studying art, but I wasn't really good at it, so after a year in Paris, I gave it up. There was a time when I wanted to become a pianist, but I was just mediocre. In photography, though, I've made quite a name for myself." She said it proudly, yet without putting too much stress on her success. "I would have made a mistake, guessing what you are," she said later. "I would never have thought of you as a lawyer. You don't look like one; you don't behave like one."

"I was all set to become a doctor."

"What made you change your mind?"

And there I was, rattling on about the firm my great-grandfather had founded, about my parents' death and how San Angelo had taken me in and what he meant to me. Justo. Clarissa. I couldn't remember ever having talked so incessantly about myself. She didn't interrupt me once, and when she moved, she moved so quietly, I failed to notice that she had cleared everything away until she set a steaming pot of coffee on the table. "Sugar?"

"No thanks. But may I smoke a pipe?"

"Do. A pipe is nice."

She watched me light it. "You should have smoked one before. The little cloud of smoke curling over your chin is just right."

We drifted back into the studio, carrying our cups of coffee. She went straight to the waterbed and stretched out on it, but when I wanted to sit down on the edge, she told me to pull up the stool on which she'd sat before. "The waterbed's only good for one. If two are on it and one of them moves, the other gets seasick."

The stool wasn't very comfortable, so I got myself one of the blue, blown-up plastic chairs, and she watched as I finally mastered it. "You've been lucky though," she said, as if we were still talking about my childhood, "in spite of all the tragedy. You had a good relationship with your parents and after that with San Angelo. I think it's very necessary to have someone you feel close to. I don't."

"Why?"

"At some point or other I always begin to feel crowded and withdrawn."

"Even as a child?"

"My mother was a beautiful woman, but cold. A stranger, really. Except for my father . . ." So it was she who brought up Butworth. It made me feel free to ask, "What kind of a man was he?"

"I remember being absolutely dependent on him," she said, staring up at the ceiling and suddenly breathing uneasily. "That was when I was little. Then . . ."

I waited quite some time before I repeated softly, "Then?"

"Oh, I'm sure it was all my fault, but he frightened me."

"Frightened you? In what way?"

"Forget it." She sounded impatient. "Anyway, I loved him. Loved him very much."

"Then his death must have been a great shock to you."

"Not so much his death as the way he died." She shuddered. "No man should die like that. Stabbed to death." Suddenly she was talking. "And the way the police searched the house. I know they had to. I'd been warned they would. There were no witnesses, you know, and no suspects. So they were trying to find out everything they could about his private life, his friends, his associates, what kind of insurance he carried. I caught one cop just as he was trying to slip one of father's notebooks in his pocket. I got it away from him. I hid most of his private papers. And all the questions! I thought I'd go mad."

No mention, I thought, about the wig or beard. She had been told about them, according to Jenkins, and must have been questioned by the police and the FBI. Was she withholding the knowledge on purpose, or was it too painful to talk about? Close or not, for any daughter or son it would have to be a terrible thing to realize that the father you knew, or believed you knew, disguised himself. There could hardly be an honest or healthy reason for it.

"I understand that he went to the opera frequently."

"Yes. He loved music. He was happy when I took up the piano and very disappointed when I gave it up. He had arranged for me to study with Nadia Boulanger in Fontainebleau. I guess I inherited my love of music from him."

"If I recall correctly, you told police that you sometimes accompanied him to Lincoln Center."

"Not sometimes. I went with him often. He asked me to go with him that night. To *Fidelio*. He had the tickets, and I stood there in the lobby, waiting for him endlessly. I was worried about him. Naturally. It was snowing, I couldn't find a taxi, and I hated taking the subway. I decided to go home. But he wasn't here either."

"Here?" I don't know why I was surprised.

"Why not? This studio and all the equipment was a present from him. He had a key to it. And sometimes, when I was away, he used it. It was more homelike than a hotel room."

That explained why the Plaza had said he never stayed there.

"I lay awake all night. And then my mother called."

A short silence. I could see Caroline in the Georgetown house, being interrogated by police. "Did he have enemies?"

"Of course."

She answered matter-of-factly, assuming, I imagined, the attitude she must have taken when questioned by the authorities.

"And what is your feeling?"

"That it was an act of revenge."

"Against the laws he upheld?"

"No. Personal," she said, without taking her eyes off the ceiling. "But what does it matter now? He is dead."

"You don't want to know?"

"I don't know. Anyway, I'm not going to. They're soft-pedaling the investigation, and maybe that's for the best."

I managed to remain silent. For a moment I doubted if

she realized what she was implying. If true, it involved a lot. The FBI contacting the State Department, the State Department contacting the mayor's office with the request to step softly, for security reasons. The mayor getting in touch with the police commissioner, he in turn calling the commanding officer at Manhattan North, and so on, all down the line: Washington wants the investigation stopped.

Why?

A couple of days ago the police commissioner had been so pleasantly ready to help me. Instead of turning me down, he had called Jenkins himself to make sure I could see him right away. And Jenkins had talked, freely, openly. I stopped short as I remembered the way he had suddenly become noncommittal when I had suggested psychics. Even his words came back to me. "We thought about it but decided against it."

I glanced at Caroline. She was lying motionless, her breathing normal again. But even by the dim light of the sconces on either side of the waterbed, I could see she was pale. There were so many questions I wanted to ask, questions I knew I mustn't ask or she would withdraw completely and possibly never want to see me again. I got up and went over to the record player. I looked through some of the Rubenstein records, found the Schubert that had more "soul," as she had said, and put it on. I pulled the chair up near the waterbed. But the music didn't help. I couldn't give myself up to it.

Why didn't Washington want the investigation to run its course? What hidden secrets in Justice Butworth's life could possibly embarrass the Administration? The wig and the beard couldn't be dismissed easily as a caprice, even a harmless idiosyncracy. Did Caroline know more? Would she tell me? I kept my eyes on her, waiting for her to feel my glance and turn to me. But she was listening attentively to the music with her eyes closed, and suddenly I saw her smile. The smile started at the corners of her mouth and did exactly what I had imagined it would do, made it soft, younger, less serious. A dimple became visible in her left cheek. It did something to her small upturned nose, what exactly I couldn't say, just that it tempted you to put a finger on the soft spot and feel the tiny cartilage move. It lingered on her high cheekbones, which were suddenly prominent. I forgot about Washington and its obscure way of handling things. I forgot that Caroline might still be living too much under the impression of the tragedy, immersing herself in her work, pushing aside everything connected with the crime. I bent over and kissed her.

She didn't respond, unless you wanted to call it a response that as soon as I withdrew my mouth, she lifted one hand to wipe the kiss off hers. She wasn't angry. She was amiable and definite. "That's not what I want, Mr. Wood. Or even like. I think you'd better go now."

I felt like a schoolboy who has just mistaken his dean's ass for that of one of his pals, and kicked it hard. I wanted to take her in my arms and stifle all her objections by kissing her passionately. I had never hesitated when sex stimulated me, but now I didn't dare to proceed with my usual technique. I didn't even try to argue the point; I didn't tell her she was behaving like a child. Didn't she know that any young man . . . and anyway, why had she let me come up, a man she didn't know, who had lied to her about an appointment? "I was almost asleep," she said. There was no reproach in her voice. "Don't bother about anything. The record player shuts off automatically, and if you slam the door real hard, it'll lock on security. But yes, there's something you could do for me. Would you put the garbage out? It's just inside the kitchen door. Thanks."

CHAPTER

NINE

Because it was sleeting, San Angelo had decided not to go out to Connecticut. Lately he seemed very conscious of the state of his health. There was a draft, the room was chilly, an electric heater should be brought in. And he was irritable. Since he was usually almost annoyingly even-tempered, the one person in the office who could calm everybody down, it worried me. Not enough though to stop me from quarreling with him. I hadn't heard from Melinda, although when I'd taken her to the airport ten days ago, she had promised to write. "Every day. I'm going to write to you every day, and please answer."

"Well, you know how children are. Out of sight, out of mind."

"But not Lindy. I don't think it was fair, San, to send her off just at Christmas time. But she'll be back next week, and I couldn't be more pleased. I wonder what she'll have to say."

"I may let her stay over there for a while. I had a long letter from her grandmother. She's picking up Italian rapidly. It's good for her to have a second language. A year of Italian schooling wouldn't do her any harm."

"She won't like it. And she'd be right to resent it. To be

sent off for a vacation and then find out you're not coming back. It's a dirty trick. You never tried anything like that on me."

"She's got to learn to adjust," said San Angelo. "She never has. Remember all the nannies we had? None of whom she liked. And later on, the governesses. She managed to run all of them out of the house. Now Miss Gilbert was a perfectly nice woman."

"She was a horror."

"Anyway, I've always given in to Linda, and I think the time has come for her to find out that everything isn't always going to go her way."

I shut up, dismayed at this sudden display of authority. He'll miss her more than she'll miss him, I thought, and in a couple of weeks he'll be sending for her. I got out the chessboard. We were evenly matched, so it was usually a challenge to play with him. One time he'd win, the next time I would. But tonight he played badly, inattentively. And he wasn't drinking his port while I refilled my glass three times. I wasn't playing too well either. I'd had a bad night, bothered by dreams in which Butworth appeared again and again, with his wig, without his wig—ridiculous stuff.

"They've stopped the investigation of Butworth's murder," I said.

San Angelo moved to protect his queen. He didn't answer, and I went on, angry that my news didn't startle him. "All this goddamn interference everywhere. The evidence is all around us but does anybody do anything about it? Noknock entry, wiretapping, all these recent conspiracy prosecutions. In every city."

"Tad!" San Angelo's fist came down so hard on the board, the little ivory figures went flying across the table. "I won't have you talking this way. You're being childish. Of course things could be better, when wasn't there a time when things couldn't have been better? But can't you be grateful for what we have? That *cum grano salis*, we're still allowed to voice our opinions, to dissent openly, to demonstrate peacefully? You talk as if you'd never heard of dictatorships. What other country allows so much freedom of speech, even open invitation to revolution? And you can leave the States if you want to. You don't have to ask for an exit permit. And be refused. Think of the millions trapped in their native land, who have to acquiesce or be imprisoned, or executed."

"But will it last? The trend is there, you can't deny it. The intrusion of government is already excessive. We could swing into totalitarianism overnight. Easily. And I'm not the only one thinking along these lines. And our last-ditch stand, San, is the law! Not law and order, but law and the order it creates, which includes, first and foremost, our freedoms."

But San Angelo, as if my news about the Butworth case had just sunk in, said, "Who told you? I mean, about Butworth."

I couldn't very well mention that Caroline, in an unguarded moment, was the source of my information. As a matter of fact, I had no intention of mentioning that I had met her. I shrugged. "I happened to hear it when I was in Washington on Friday."

"Possibly just a rumor. Anything to discredit the Administration. Probably put out by some of the people you like to run around with. People with no perspective and no constructive plan. I wouldn't listen to them, Tad. And I wouldn't repeat it either."

"But he was a close friend of the President, an adviser. So when they stop the investigation . . ."

"I'm sure it's a fabrication," San Angelo said and, for the first time, reached for his glass and swallowed the contents in one gulp. When he put the glass down, there was a little drop of the red liquid left on his lower lip. It looked like blood. "This damn sensationalism. The truth is never enough. It's one of the worst characteristics of our nation. Worse than drugs, if you ask me. Drugs only harm the person who takes them, but rumors . . ."

The comparison wasn't exactly correct. Didn't he realize how many muggings, how many murders were committed to get a fix to say nothing of the tragedy for those lovingly involved with the addict?

"Furthermore," he went on, "why in the world should you busy yourself with things like this? It has nothing to do with your job on the commission. Stay away from it."

"You knew him," I said. "I always meant to ask you what sort of an impression he made on you."

"I knew him, yes, but very slightly. He came up to the house a few times, but he wasn't a man one got to know. Tight-lipped. An introvert." He smiled. "And even for me, too much of a law and order man. *His* idea of law and order."

Ordinarily he would have described the man at length. Obviously he had no intention of doing so now. I tried to prod him again. "His will is up for probation next week. I wonder how much he left."

"I wouldn't be surprised if it was quite a bit. He was a corporation lawyer before he went in for political appointments. But I'm sure it's all above board."

And that was all I could get out of him. Perhaps if I told him about the wig and the beard, it might startle him into revealing some more information, if he had any. "Then why," I asked, "did he disguise himself?"

"Disguise himself?"

"Yes. He wore a wig and a beard. At times."

San Angelo changed color, or so it seemed to me. "How do you know?"

I didn't want to tell him that I'd seen Lieutenant Jenkins. I shrugged.

"Rumor, too," said San Angelo. "Just another one of those damn fabrications. I'm convinced it isn't true. Come on, let's have our game."

He helped me to pick up the figures from the floor, and as we set up the board again, I noticed that his hands were trembling. We played one more game, which San Angelo

won, but he was too tired to give me a return match. I left
him when he had finished his cigar. It was still early.
Around midnight. There was nobody waiting for me at
home, nobody I could call, so I went to a movie. A Truffaut
picture. I guess it was good but it failed to distract me.
Butworth, Jenkins, Caroline, Melinda—all of them appeared on the screen of my mind, more real than what was
being played out in front of me. Then I went into a bar on
Third Avenue. But I've never enjoyed drinking by myself
and there wasn't anybody in the rather crowded restaurant
who looked worth talking to. I took a taxi home. By that
time it was three o'clock, or a little later, but as I stuck my
key in the door, I heard my telephone ringing.

It was Caroline. "I hope I didn't wake you up," she said,
"but you told me you always read late into the night."

"Wonderful to hear your voice," I said, trying to catch my
breath and push the dog away at the same time.

"Do you have your car outside?"

I didn't, but I said yes. "I just came in and I haven't called
my garage yet."

"That's good," she said. "Could you come over right
away?"

"I'll be there as fast as I can." And then I caught a strange
little sound, like someone swallowing a sob. Caroline hadn't
impressed me as someone who would cry over the telephone, but then I hadn't figured her either as a girl who
would call up a man in the middle of the night. "Is anything
wrong? Are you all right?"

"I'm fine now," she said, and hung up.

I whistled for Tiger. There wasn't a taxi in sight. I finally
found one on Eighth Avenue. A drunk was trying to get out
of it. He couldn't find his change, then found a twenty dollar bill and put it back, brought up a handful of coins, not
enough, and stuffed them back into his pocket, and all the
time I was hearing that strange little sob, so gallantly sup-
pressed. In the end I paid his fare.

At a hundred and forty-nine East Nineteenth Street, the

front door opened after my first buzz. Tiger jumped ahead of me, waiting at each landing to make sure I was following him. Her door stood ajar as it had done the first time I'd come, but this time unchained. I could hear the record player, but I couldn't see her. It was Tiger who spotted her, and gave a loud bark. She was lying slumped on the floor in the kitchen, under the wall phone. The receiver was dangling from it and there was blood on the tiled floor and on the wall. A gash on her forehead was open.

There was an ice cube machine; she'd shown it to me only two days ago, so it was easy to gather up some cubes in my hand. I put them in my handkerchief, then on her forehead. After a couple of minutes she came to. "Easy now," I said. I went into the studio and grabbed a cushion. "Lie back. Here. On the cushion. Don't try to say anything yet."

I found the medicine cabinet in the bathroom, and the gauze I'd been looking for. I stuffed it into the open wound. There was some coffee left in the chemex, carefully covered with a plate. I poured it into a pan to heat it, then I brought her a cup. "I'd rather have you sit up again while you drink this. If you can." I put my arm around her and braced her, counting the sips she took. Color was coming back to her cheeks and I decided to move her. I carried her into the studio and laid her down gently on the waterbed, found a blanket and covered her. Then I noticed a little pool of water near the door in the left wall, and a trace of it all along the floor to the kitchen. When I closed the door to the narrow balcony outside the studio, she said, "He must have come over the roof."

"Your head needs attention," I told her. "You can tell me later. Who's your doctor?"

"He's out of town," she said. "I called him before I called you. It's Sunday, you know." Her voice was barely audible, but she seemed to be all right.

"As soon as you feel equal to it, I'll take you to the hospital."

"I'm not going to any hospital," she said, with some of the

old firmness in her voice. She watched me pick up the phone. "And don't dial police," she told me, anticipating my next move. "I don't want police either."

"But . . ."

"I don't want any publicity on this. None whatsoever."

I obeyed because I could see the headlines. DAUGHTER OF MURDERED JUSTICE ATTACKED, and dialed another number.

"Who are you calling now?"

"A friend of mine who happens to be a doctor."

Hackett had just finished his internship at Bellevue and set up his own practice. He was home. "Does she have a concussion?"

"How can I tell?"

"Is she vomiting? Does she complain of a headache? Any blurred vision?"

"For God's sake, concussion or not, she's got a finger-wide gash in her forehead and she's bleeding. Get your ass over here."

"No," he said. "I don't know what I may need. Bring her to my office. Stuff up that wound and see she doesn't fall. As little motion as possible."

When she said she thought she could make it, I went downstairs to find a taxi. This time I was lucky. A gypsy cab came along before I had rounded the corner. I told the man to come up and help me carry someone down. "Jeez," he said. "You don't look like the kind of guy who beats up dames."

Hackett's office was on Eighty-third Street in a professional building. I don't know how often I told the driver to take it easy, to avoid bumps, to drive slowly. About the sixth time, he turned around angrily. "You don't think I want my bus full of that juice. Blood doesn't wash out easily and I don't want any questions."

"Jean Smith," Caroline said when she met Hackett, then she passed out again. I didn't contradict her. He sewed her up, x-rayed her, and finally said it looked okay to him.

Maybe a concussion would manifest itself later, she might start to vomit, the main thing was to keep her quiet and in bed for at least three days, to call him if there were any complications, otherwise to come back in a week's time so he could take out the stitches. That he'd given her some kind of shot or other, and yes, he had his car outside. Could he give us a lift home?

"I'm not going to let you go back to your apartment and be there all by yourself," I told her, while Hackett was getting his car. "I'm taking you home with me."

I had expected her to object, but she merely said, "Thank you." And there she was, lying on my couch as if she'd always lain there. Even her bandaged head didn't look strange to me. I built a fire, and after I had it going, poured myself a drink. She wasn't supposed to have any liquor, just sips of water, and I brought the ice container over to the low table between the couch and the fireplace. And poured myself another drink.

"San Angelo would say I'm behaving like a Jewish nurse," I told her, in an effort to cheer her up a little. "You're the patient, but I'm the one who's suffering." She let it go for the lame joke it was. "You know," she said presently, "I called you because I thought, as a lawyer, you'd understand better than anyone else why I didn't want an ambulance or the emergency ward in a hospital. Or police."

I would have liked to know whom else she might have called, but other things seemed more important than my sudden curiosity about the relationships she might have with other men. That there were some would be only natural.

"I must have dozed off," she said, talking more to herself than to me, "then suddenly I felt a draft. The door to the balcony stood ajar. I thought it had blown open. It does sometimes, with the wind in the right direction. But then I heard a noise. There was a man in my lab. I could see him through the open door. He was trying to open the safe. It's under the sink. You wouldn't notice it unless you knew. It's an old-fashioned safe and he couldn't operate the wheel. Next he tried to jack it out from under the enamel cover that makes it look like something the water from the sink runs into. I pretended to be asleep. My father taught me that. Don't get panicky, don't yell for help or get up and try to run away. What thieves fear most is to be recognized. That's when they may kill. So I lay very still. He went through my desk and all the drawers in every piece of furniture. He was careful to put everything back. Then he opened my closet and looked in every pocket."

She stopped speaking, as if it had exhausted her, but she soon started again. "I must have made a move, something that attracted his attention. He came over to the bed, and suddenly I was afraid, terribly afraid, and I sat up as if I had just awakened, and rubbed my eyes. That's when he hit me over the head. I think it was a blackjack, but I'm not sure. I've never heard of thieves carrying blackjacks. Knives, yes, and guns, or iron pipes."

"Would you recognize him?"

"I think so."

"What did he look like?"

But she made a little movement with her head as if she wanted to wave my question away, so I tried another. "What do you think he was after?"

"Dope," she said. "Or money to buy dope."

"Did he take any of your cameras?"

"I don't know. The last thing I saw was that blackjack bearing down on me."

"We'll find out tomorrow. You make a list and I'll go over there and check."

"Whatever he took, I don't want to claim it. I don't want it to come out that I was broken into and robbed."

I let a few minutes pass to give her a rest, then I asked, "Caroline, are you sure he was only after dope or money?"

She sipped some water. "What else?"

"Do you suppose he could have been after your father's notebook or some of his private papers? You said you hid them."

"I burned them."

"Good," I said, and never spoke a bigger lie. I would have given a lot to see those papers. Nor was I sure she was telling the truth.

After a little while I showed her the bathroom, then helped her upstairs. I opened the zipper of her dress for her and tactfully found something to do which made it necessary to turn my back, but when I heard her rustle with the covers, I went over to her and tucked her in. "I'll be sleeping downstairs," I said. "On the couch. If you need anything, I've brought up this little bell. If I don't hear it, Tiger will."

"I like him," she said. "Come here, Tiger. You haven't bothered me once." As she turned, her glance fell on a photo next to my bed. Melinda. "Oh," she said. "She's beautiful. Who is she?"

I told her about Melinda.

"Beautiful," she said again. "She'll give men a hard time some day. What was her name again? Melinda," and then, unexpectedly, she dropped off. When I was sure she was asleep, I went downstairs, made myself some coffee, got some linen and a pillow and bedded myself down in front of the fire for what was left of the night. I drank all the coffee I had made, which was more than three cups, because I had no intention of dozing off. I had a lot of thinking to do.

CHAPTER

TEN

CAROLINE SLEPT the sleep of someone completely exhausted. "And," said Rose, "she cries in her sleep."

Rose had volunteered to stay in my apartment until I got home in the evening. "No sobbing, nothing like that, but when I run up to see if she's all right there's tears on her cheeks. And she doesn't even wake up when I wipe them away."

Once, when she woke, I offered to move to a hotel. "If I bother you," she said. "But you'll leave me the dog, won't you? With Tiger here, I wouldn't be afraid."

Tiger wouldn't move out of my bedroom. Except for food and a quick walk, he lay on the floor at the foot of the bed, growling softly—as if he knew better than to rouse her—whenever anybody entered. On the fourth day she seemed a little stronger, and I brought my after-dinner coffee up to her. "You said you would recognize the man. Did you see him so clearly before he hit you?"

"I saw him clearly most of the time he was there, while I was pretending to be asleep." She touched her forehead. "This damn headache. You know, it's funny, but I have a feeling I've seen him before. But I can't remember when or where. I can't place him. It's odd. I usually remember a face, not names, but faces. And how people walk."

"Don't try too hard," I told her. "It'll come back."

She gave me a list of her equipment, and her key. I went over to her apartment, picked up the few things she wanted and made a thorough check. Nothing was missing except a small Kodak movie camera. "He must have taken it before I noticed him," said Caroline.

I went to see Lieutenant Jenkins and told him about it. This time one of his detectives was present and took down everything I said, but both men agreed that the thief undoubtedly had been after money or drugs. And that Miss Butworth was lucky he hadn't taken more. Someone was sent over to take fingerprints, but Caroline refused to go to the rogue's gallery and try to identify the man from photos, when I repeated Jenkins' suggestion, pretending it was my own, because I didn't want her to know I'd talked to police. Without asking her permission, I called the Holmes service and had alarms put on every door. It would be a nuisance to have to call the service every time she opened her front door or the little door to the balcony, but it made me feel easier. "Maybe you should move," I told her. "There aren't any back stairs, just that flimsy fire escape, and that's none too safe. I tried it."

"It's hard to find a studio," she said. "I looked for a long time before I found mine. For instance, yours would never do. Too little light." As if I had offered her my quarters. It was a strange characteristic of hers, taking all sorts of things for granted, on the other hand, so polite and considerate.

"That girl's crazy," Rose said, the day the stitches were taken out. "She had me buy a whole pound of caviar, and you know what that costs nowadays. Just because I said you like it. She gave me some of it, quite a lot, when I asked her what it tasted like, since I'd never come closer to it than putting it in the icebox. Well, it's fishy all right, and gluey, sorta like peanuts. It sits on your tongue and you want more. And look at the flowers. All over the place. She's crazy about flowers, but now I've got to run around and cut their stems, half an inch, she said, and no fresh water, just fill up what they've drunk during the night. Did you know that flowers drink most at night?"

"Well, she'll be moving back to her own place any day now," I said.

Rose straightened her glasses, which were always threatening to fall off her nose. "You're crazy, Mr. Tad. Wouldn't be fun to come here and find her gone. You keep her, listen to me, man. That is, if she'll have you."

But she wouldn't have me. During all those days there hadn't been a gesture on her part to indicate I was welcome to try to kiss her again. That night we had the caviar, with all the trimmings, finely chopped parsley, egg yolk and egg white and onions and crisp toast and quantities of lemon. I asked her to marry me. It was the first time I heard her really laugh. Loud and long. I didn't feel flattered. "What's so funny?"

"You," she said, "or rather, the idea of marrying. Me and marrying! I'll never marry."

"Every girl says that."

"I'm not every girl. I mean it."

"And why not?"

Suddenly she was serious. Her mouth drooped and she put her spoon back into the little crystal bowl that she had stood in ice, to keep the roe cold.

"Was your parents' marriage so bad? Did you suffer under it?"

"No. I never heard them quarrel. Maybe they did, but never in front of me. They were always polite and apparently considerate of each other. But there was never any tenderness between them, and I think that was my mother's fault, because he had a great deal of warmth. My friends adored him."

"Don't you want any children?"

"Children?" she repeated, and dragged out the word as if I had proposed a new population explosion. "Definitely not. No. No children for me."

"Were you an unhappy child?"

"On the contrary. I was very happy. My parents were wise enough to leave me alone. I don't mean by that that they were overly permissive. They insisted on manners, which I can't remember ever having resented. I had my duties to perform—keep my room tidy, my bike shiny. I took piano and dancing lessons and brought home fairly decent report cards, but otherwise . . ." She shook her head. There were two lines along the scar where Hackett had had to shave her hair to treat the wound. Lighter than the rest of her close-cropped curls, they reminded me of a little bird, still wet and naked, before it grew its first feathers. I wanted to touch them. Badly. Just run my finger over them.

"Then what have you got against children and marriage?"

She took a long time answering. Finally she said, "I think it's just that I really don't like men."

I stared at her. "You like women better?"

"Lord, no," she said. "I detest females."

I poured her another Aquavit. Yes, I had been buying Aquavit lately. "So you had a dreadful experience with a man that left you shattered and disgusted."

"Hold it," she said, draining her glass. "I haven't known a man. Sorry to horrify you. But as yet I've had . . . I haven't been together yet with a man."

All I could do was stammer, "That isn't possible! How old are you?"

"Twenty-three," she said, and laughed.

"A virgin? I don't believe it."

She shrugged. "There are worse things. And it isn't all that impossible."

"But you told me you traveled with that Swede, the writer . . ."

"Per?"

"That's it. Per Gunnarsen. You traveled with him for almost half a year to God knows where. Greece, wasn't it? Photographing the places he was writing about."

"I did. What does that have to do with sleeping?"

"Don't tell me he never tried."

"Of course he tried. But he's a European. European men don't have the kind of inferiority complex Americans have. You can tell them, no thank you, and they don't come back with 'What's wrong with me?' He knew there was nothing wrong with him. The first time he asked me out of politeness, the second time because he had nothing better to do. But it didn't put him off. He continued to give me a chance to be published with him and I was grateful. I sewed his buttons back on his pajamas, made scrambled eggs for him in the middle of the night, things like that. We're still the best of friends."

"I don't understand you. There was nobody when you were in college?"

"No."

"And when you were studying in Paris?"

"No."

Her hand touched mine, fleetingly, the first time she had ever touched me. "Don't look so appalled. I'm really quite normal. Maybe I'm just not very sexy."

"And there's nobody now?"

"Come on, Tad. Would I be here if there were? No. There's nobody now."

"And I don't count either."

"Yes," she said. "You count. In my book you count. But not as a prospective lover or husband. Sorry if you gave up your bed and slept on a couch without getting what you hoped for. What would you think of my moving to a hotel as soon as I can find something I like and can afford? And I'd use my studio only as a place to work."

The subject of sex, I could see, was closed.

"There's one thing I've been meaning to ask you all these days—was there a lot of hate mail? I mean"—and I was careful how I phrased it—"did your father get many threatening letters?"

"Yes," she said. "But Dad's outer office usually coped with it. I think that's where they're filed. Or the Secret Intelligence Service took care of them. I never paid much attention to it; Dad didn't either. The President and Vice President and some Senators got more. I only remember when there was a threat to kidnap me. Then Dad got worried. I wasn't allowed out alone, suddenly the house was a fortress, with wires all over the place, and alarms. The cat kept setting them off and everybody was in a foul mood because police would arrive and you had to placate them, make them coffee, give them drinks, feed them. For a while two men lived with us. We called them Pat and Patachon."

She put up her legs and lay back. "And then they got Dad. Dad, who never took a threat seriously. The medical examiner said he must have died right away. I hope so." She shivered. "What's the Brevoort like? Or is One Fifth Avenue better? Both are frightfully expensive. Maybe I can find a pad closer to the studio. That's what I'd really like. But most of the hotels there are fleabags."

Again she slept upstairs and I, near the fireplace, on the couch. Not very well though. The lilies she had bought smelled too strongly and I had to put them in the kitchen or they'd have given me a headache. And anyhow, I couldn't get over what she had told me. I didn't believe that she was still a virgin. At twenty-three? She must have lied. For God knows what reasons. Maybe, I thought, before I finally fell asleep, I was too American after all. But I was also too much of a man to forget that the girl was in danger, a danger I couldn't pinpoint yet. The investigation into Justice Butworth's murder had been stopped, but evidently there was somebody who didn't know about it or didn't care, and was proceeding on his own.

CHAPTER

ELEVEN

I SAID TO MRS. JOHNSON, "I understand there was a lot of hate mail. Maybe we should look into it. It might give some of our learned experts a new approach on how to deal with terror as a measure to fight unpopular laws."

"I felt all along that you should have got in touch with the FBI. They're not as inefficient or secretive as you think."

As far as I could recall, I hadn't voiced any opinion on the FBI and I greeted the young man who came to my office in a way I considered cordial. He was a lanky fellow, rather staid, like the guys on photos after World War II. Neat. Crew cut. In his manner modest, almost obsequious in spite of his arrogant smile. He didn't drink, he didn't smoke. He gave me the impression that he'd joined the FBI, as so many did, to make connections, to meet people who might come in handy at a future date in whatever branch he eventually chose for a career. My guess was real estate. He had that look.

His name was Momford, and I told him I wanted the complete file of hate mail received by Justice Butworth throughout his career. Presto. I pored over it for several nights before I passed it on to an appropriate man on the commission. It was incredible to read how men could vent their pent-up hatreds and frustrations in letters. At times the language was obscene, so obscene it made you physically sick. Sometimes it made sense up to a point at which all logic was abandoned and the writer became a raving maniac. Then again one had to admire the courage, the idealism, occasionally even the farsightedness. But all in all it was extremely distressing and I could well understand that anyone receiving that kind of mail wouldn't want to look at it, but would file it away as a matter of procedure. I read and reread the threat to kidnap Caroline. "We'll tie her to a pole, tar and feather her, and every man passing her will rape her, like they raped the women at the gates of Rome. And if she isn't dead by six in the morning, we'll kill her." There was another letter, though, which I found interesting. It accused Butworth of a too lenient attitude toward a gambling outfit run by the Mafia. "They should have got the electric chair for all the people they killed when they couldn't pay back the credit extended to them. But you reversed the conviction. Why? We know. We know that you frequented that boarded-up store. You're one of them. Try to deny it. One day one of their officers will sing and you'll be known for what you are. A crook. A murderer. Using your office to enrich yourself."

I went through record after record of the period when Butworth had been an appellate judge. It was true, he had reversed the sentence of a man called Tomato, because of his red hair, who had later committed suicide.

"Caroline, every man has some vice or other. Didn't your father have any?"

"Oh, Tad, let the dead rest. You know I don't like to talk about him."

"No vices?"

"Golf," she said. "He used to play golf with the President, and with others, even alone, any time he could fit it in."

"In New York?"

"Come on, can't you be serious?" And after a pause—"He liked to take long hot baths. He had a telephone installed in the bathroom. He took a lot of calls there. He loved to lie in hot, scented water."

"Caroline! He was stabbed in a vicious way. Your apartment was broken into. Whoever it was . . . what do you think he was looking for?"

"I haven't the slightest idea."

"What do you know about your father and don't want to tell?"

"I told you, I know nothing more about him. After all, I didn't spy on him. Why should I? I trusted him. He had a right to live his life as he saw fit."

"Why do you think Washington stopped the investigation?"

"Ask them. I don't know. And I have no intention of speculating about it. I lost a father I loved. And nothing anybody may find out will bring him back to life. He can't defend himself anymore, so I don't want to see him accused of anything."

"It's because of you, because you're . . ."

But she interrupted me. "Tad. Don't lie so blatantly. You were interested long before you met me. As a matter of fact, as you said, you looked me up because of your obsession with the case."

"You said your father frightened you once. How?"

"I don't remember."

"Who was the man?"

"What man?"

"Christ! Your hair hasn't even grown back yet. The man who hit you over the head."

"Oh, he."

"You said you had the feeling you'd seen him before. You said you'd try to remember."

"Well, I still don't."

We were in her studio, I on the waterbed, which I'd

adopted as the most comfortable resting place, pliable as a woman, she on the floor, rummaging through some photographs she had taken before I knew her. I was looking down, watching her put some on a discard pile, others, according to date, into folders. She was fumbling around with one, apparently not sure where to file it, when I spotted a familiar face. "Hey, what's that? Give it to me." I almost tore it out of her hand. Unmistakably, it was Melinda.

"How in the world . . ."

She took it from me, looked at it, nodded. "I knew I'd seen that girl before, and I was right. It bothered me . . ."

She handed the glossy back to me. It was typical of Melinda, hair blowing in her face, mouth wide open as if drinking in life. "When on earth did you take it?"

"Turn it around."

The date was on the back. January. A year ago. She had been eleven.

"It must have been when I was shooting a series in the park," Caroline said. "Sunday in Central Park. A sort of *people on Sunday*. Do you remember that German picture? Well, it was so old, one could pick up the idea again. And that girl struck me . . ."

"It couldn't have been a Sunday. We're always in Connecticut on Sundays."

"Very possibly not. I shot for two or three weeks, off and on, before I put them together. She skated beautifully."

"And I'm right behind her. See?"

She took the picture from me. "So you are. You've aged since then. What happened?"

"Work." I glanced over her shoulder. I did look younger. "I taught her how to skate. Yes, she's good at it."

"You're in love with her," said Caroline.

It was the first remark she'd ever made about any relationship of mine with other people, the first time she showed any curiosity, something I'd come to appreciate as interest. But I didn't care for this observation. "In love? The

girl was twelve on her last birthday. I love her, yes. She's
Clarissa and Justo's daughter. I told you, didn't I? She's very
lovable. Of course I love her, like the little sister I never
had."

She tore up the photo, slowly, thoughtfully. "Tad," she
said, "don't you think it would be better if we didn't see so
much of each other?"

"If you don't like my company . . ."

"There we go again," she said. "For once I'm trying to
show consideration and you react like a fool. It can't be
healthy for you not to be sleeping with a girl."

"Who tells you I'm not?"

"Relax," she said, and handed me a cigarette. "You don't
have to show off. It doesn't matter to me whether you are or
not. The trouble with you is you have such a one-track mind
—I could scream."

"So scream."

To my utter surprise, she did. Long and loud. And after
that we laughed. And what could have turned into a quarrel
or, worse, endless discussion, became a joke. That was the
kind of girl she was, and one of the reasons I loved her,
although it certainly was the strangest love affair I'd ever
conducted, with a girl who refused to recognize the thrill
and satisfaction of sex. Perhaps, if I had thought it through
at the time, I might have found the key to her attitude,
might have realized before it was almost too late, that the
one thing she was really afraid of was the power of sex. I
left her when I had finished my cigarette. She hadn't found
a hotel that suited her and had moved back to her studio.
"Since you had all that expensive hardware installed," meaning the Holmes service, "I'm well enough protected."

I didn't share her feeling of security. I said to Mrs. Johnson, "I can't understand our police. They're not doing their
job. I talked to Lieutenant Jenkins yesterday, and there's
nothing new on Butworth. I thought by now they might
have called in a psychic."

Mrs. Johnson took a Q-tip out of her ear, examined it, and threw it in the wastepaper basket. "You mean a medium?" And she started in on a case she had heard about. Murder stories interested her no end.

"I don't want a medium."

"I see. You want a psychic. The best ones are in California or Europe. You could always fly to Los Angeles if Snipe didn't work out. But he's supposed to be excellent. Walter Snipe. Ever heard of him?"

Snipe? No. I hadn't heard of him. Nor did I want to ask Lieutenant Jenkins about him. I don't know if I nodded, but when I came back from lunch there was a note on my desk. Walter Snipe. And his address, just across from Hammacher Schlemmer. Fourth floor, apartment B. Five o'clock tomorrow afternoon. What more could you possibly ask of a secretary?

CHAPTER

TWELVE

WALTER SNIPE. Mrs. Johnson hadn't warned me, or perhaps she hadn't known. He was a dwarf. And when he opened the door, I didn't see him at first and thought it must have been opened by some mechanical device. Then I heard his voice. It came fluting up from below me, a perfect soprano. "Come in, Mr. Wood. To the right. Follow me, please." He led the way through a rather dark passage into a small, well-lit room. Every piece of furniture was built in accordance with his height—tables, chairs, writing desk—except for one standard size armchair near the window. He pointed to it.

"Tea?" he asked. "I have it ready."

His face was marvelously proportioned, with a wide, slightly curved forehead, an almost aquiline nose and a determined, clefted chin. His eyes, set wide apart from the nose, reminded me of San Angelo's. Alert, like those of a deer, with the melancholy of an animal. He wore his hair shoulder length. It was iron gray and made his head appear bigger than it was.

He served tea on an oblong, red lacquered Japanese tray. Jasmine tea, the delicate flavor of which I liked. On the tray there were cookies, obviously homemade—they tasted odd

—and a banana. I was lifting one of the thin little cups when, from above, came a sound I mistook at first for the twitter of a bird. But down from the curtain rod rushed a little monkey, a white-throated Capuchin with a prehensile tail at least twenty inches long, and a beard. In one of San Angelo's stories about his childhood, his father had had a monkey like this on his cart.

The Capuchin grabbed the banana, began to peel it neatly and speedily, took a bite, then threw it down and jumped on my lap and from there to the crook of my elbow. It reached out one long, thin arm, took hold of my hair and with an almost caressing gesture, patted my cheek.

"Mr. Chips is partial to color," said Snipe. "Now if you'd had black hair, he might have slapped your face."

The monkey let the little tuft of hair it had pulled out from just above my forehead fall to the floor and went back to his place at the table to finish his banana. We talked for a while about monkeys and how easy it was to keep them if the temperature was right and one fed them correctly. The monkey had been a present from a grateful client. Then, quite abruptly, Snipe looked up. "What can I do for you, Mr. Wood?"

I told him about Justice Butworth's assassination and some of the circumstances under which he had been found. Actually only what was public knowledge, nothing of what Lieutenant Jenkins and Caroline had revealed. "I wonder if you could possibly find it in your power to see who killed him."

"I'll try," said Snipe. "But I must warn you . . . I'm not always successful. It all depends."

"On what?"

"In my case, on God. If God wills it . . ."

There was no hocus-pocus, no closing of curtains or switching off of lights, no crystal ball, no clearing away of dishes for complete order. Snipe remained seated in his child-size chair, closed his eyes and folded his hands, finger-

tips against fingertips, like a Hindu welcoming a guest. He
held himself absolutely motionless until he began to look
like a lifeless figure rather than a human being. I watched
him for a while, then let my eyes wander around the room.
Shelves, filled from top to bottom with books on almost
every kind of religion. On the floor and windowsills, plants,
some tree high, mostly cacti and palms and one small linden
tree, right next to me, its branches strung on wires. When I
looked at Snipe after what I gathered to be a good half
hour, his face was white, and he seemed to be barely breathing. But the most startling thing about him was his hands.
He was still holding them in the same position. When I had
looked at them before, I had thought how extraordinarily
beautiful they were, how slim the fingers. Now they were
twice, if not three times their original size, they were that
swollen. And they too looked lifeless and frighteningly
white. Then, as I watched, the swelling began to subside.
When they were their normal size again, Snipe opened his
eyes, but for a few minutes he didn't seem to see me. Sweat
was pouring down his high forehead and standing in shiny
drops on his upper lip, even his gaily striped shirt was wet.
And when he spoke, his voice was hoarse, as if he were
suffering from a throat ailment.

As casually as if we were conducting a quite ordinary
conversation, he said, "An inquiry into Justice Butworth's
murder is still going on. A third party is interested in dis-
covering what led to his death."

He swallowed, and when he continued, after a short
pause, his voice was clear again. "The murderer lives between Fifth Avenue and Madison. East Seventy-seventh
Street, number five. I can't see the murderer, nor does his
name come to me. I'm sorry, but I can't give you any more
details." He repeated the address, and when I looked for a
piece of paper to jot it down and couldn't find one, he gave
me one of his cards.

It was only when I began to write that the realization

stunned me. It was the street in which San Angelo lived, the house in which he had his apartment. The pencil began to tremble in my hands and I dropped the card. Snipe picked it up for me. "Are you . . . are you sure this is the correct address?"

"It is the address I was allowed to see," he said, "as for its being correct . . ." He shrugged, then suddenly leaned forward, and peering into my eyes, asked, "But *why* must *you* find out?"

"Maybe I won't."

"It would be better if you didn't."

"Why do you say that?"

"I told you that a third party was interested. Besides, no one should occupy himself with something for which he is not chosen."

"Somehow I feel compelled."

Perhaps I was just answering myself, justifying what Caroline called my obsession with her father's case. How could I explain the compulsion that drove me to solve Butworth's murder?

"I have to feed the monkey now," said Snipe, cradling the Capuchin in his arms. "Call me if you want to. You know, sometimes a piece of clothing can be of great help, something the deceased possessed, or a suspect . . ."

It was almost an invitation to come back, and it made his advice not to get further involved seem foolish, and somehow hypocritical. Suddenly I was sure that he had seen more in his trance, but was not revealing it to me, and I would have liked to sit down and question him further, but he had got out of his chair and was already at the door. "I'll see you again soon," I said.

"I don't think you will."

"Oh, but I must. And please send your bill to my office."

"No fee," he said, and when I looked surprised, wondering how he could afford not to charge for his services, he added, as if reading my mind, "I'm a psychologist. Or didn't you

know? And I have a very good practice. Good night." Then
suddenly, as if he had forgotten to mention it before, he
said, "Look for a dark-haired man."

I was supposed to have dinner with San Angelo, and I
decided to walk the twenty blocks. We had a complicated
contract to work out, between two merging firms, and I
should have been concentrating on some of the problems
that had manifested themselves only today, but I couldn't
keep my mind on them. San Angelo's street. San Angelo's
apartment house. Six other parties lived in that house, besides the janitor and his family in the basement. Any one of
them might be involved, yet as I recalled what I knew about
them, not one seemed to come even remotely into question.
Snipe must have been wrong.

I grew aware that I was being followed only at around
Sixtieth Street. The awareness came gradually. It started
between my shoulder blades, a shiver running across a lim-
ited area of flesh, such as one has before coming down with
a cold. It spread gradually to the back of my neck, a feeling
of being pricked by a small, sharp instrument. I'd never
been trailed in my life. I stopped at the lighted showcase of
a bookshop and pretended to be reading some of the titles
displayed as I watched the street. Fairly empty since the
stores were already closed. Two cops strolling on the opposite side, swinging their nightsticks; a nurse, in a hurry, her
shoes white under a street lamp. A blind man and his seeing-
eye dog, feeling his way. A man with a briefcase, waiting at
a bus stop. Two women trying to hail a taxi. The usual
thing. I turned. Casually. There was no one behind me. I
walked on. Why should anybody be following me? Why
should my moves be important to a third person? I thought
of the man who had broken into Caroline's apartment, the
brutality with which he had hit her over the head. What did
she possess that someone else wanted? And did this someone
else think I was involved? I quickened my pace.

At Seventy-second Street there was a group of schoolchildren. At an hour, I thought, when school had been over long ago. Behind them I could see a long, lanky fellow. He seemed hesitant as to where to walk next. I turned when he did and there he was, on the opposite side of the street. It was Momford, the FBI man Mrs. Johnson had called when I'd wanted the files of the hate mail Butworth had received while in office.

"Hello," he said. "I was just trying to find a place to have a bite. Why don't you keep me company?"

"Dinner by yourself? I thought you were married."

"Divorced. Three weeks ago. I thought she'd never let it go through."

I didn't have him down for a man who would divorce his wife. He'd looked too steady, too conventional. "Any children?"

"Thank God, no. Couldn't have afforded to move to a hotel with a kid. It's too expensive as it is, but I can't find an apartment."

"Sorry. I have an appointment."

I moved on, but the feeling of being followed moved with me. I stopped at Schrafft's, at the corner of Seventy-seventh Street, and stood for a few minutes facing the house in which San Angelo lived, as if seeing it for the first time. A narrow building. No doorman. Whoever was elevator man doubled for the guy who opened taxi doors or saw occupants to the cab he'd hailed for them. San Angelo had wanted to rent the penthouse, but had finally taken the only apartment available, a duplex on the ground floor. His door was next to that of the elevator, and they were frequently mistaken for each other. A steady annoyance to his servants.

"Good evening, Mr. Wood."

A voice behind me. I almost jumped, then swung around and faced the boy standing next to me. A slight, slim youngster. Doug. Melinda's temporarily discarded boyfriend. He lived next door.

"Hi, Doug. What's this business of calling me Mr. Wood?"

He grinned, embarrassed. "Long time no see." And then, "I stopped you because I haven't heard from Lindy since she left. Nobody has. I thought she was only going to stay two weeks. When is she coming back?"

"I don't know."

"You haven't got her address by any chance? Mr. San Angelo promised to let me have it, but I haven't been able to get hold of him."

It sounded like a reproach, and suddenly it occurred to me that by sending Melinda away over the holidays, yet another Christmas had been spoiled for Doug. Years ago, his parents had let him down. Badly. Coming home from school with two pals he had invited for the vacation, he had found himself locked out and finally been told by the doorman that his parents had gone off on a cruise and given the maids the time off, and that he had no key to let him in. I couldn't remember how San Angelo had heard about it, but that was how we got to know Doug that evening, angry, humiliated and forlorn, and how his friendship with Melinda had started.

I gave him the address, and he shook my hand so hard, I thought it would come off. "See you," I said, and watched him disappear into his house before I went into ours and rang the bell to San Angelo's apartment.

Riley took my coat, and San Angelo and I had a quick drink before going in to dinner. Already at dinner we began to discuss the merger agreement, and when I tried to distract him by asking about Melinda, he waved my question away with one of his sweeping motions. "Later." But later he sat down to the papers he'd brought home from the office and already spread out on his desk in the library. We worked until nearly midnight, then he seemed very tired. He asked me to sleep there; as far as he was concerned, the room was still mine. "I've got to take Tiger out."

"Oh, yes, your damned dog."

He didn't like dogs; Tiger didn't like him either. He never felt welcome. "Any particular reason why you wanted me to stay?" Perhaps there was something on his mind. Like so many people, San Angelo, once undressed and comfortable in one of his old dressing gowns, would open up over a nightcap. Our best talks had taken place that way. Even in my childhood, when he'd come into Justo's and my room, we munching Eskimo pies, our Coca-Cola bottles on the floor, watching television, he with his good-night cigar. He'd turn off the television and settle down in the rocker. "Well now, boys . . ." But tonight he shook his head and said a little too sharply, "No, no."

I hesitated. He noticed it and added, "No reason whatsoever."

"Good night, then." I sneezed and told myself how silly I had been to imagine I was being trailed a few hours ago when all I had felt were the first warnings of a cold. As I pulled out my handkerchief, Snipe's card came out with it, and since I was still standing beside the desk, it fell directly in front of San, face down. "You've lost something," he said. Nothing escaped his attention. Without the slightest sign of discretion, he turned the card over and read it, then read it again.

"Walter Snipe?" he said. "What the hell could you possibly have to do with Walter Snipe?"

"You've heard of him?"

"Who hasn't?"

Now it was out of the question that San Angelo should ever have used a man like Snipe. He rejected categorically any aspects of the occult, and psychoanalysis. Professionally, therefore, there would never have been a reason to see Snipe. Not the way our firm was conducted. We didn't even handle divorce cases, unless it was an old client. That's how stodgy we were.

"Butworth left almost a million dollars," I said. "That's quite a sum for a Justice."

"That's why you went to see Snipe?"

"I'm increasingly convinced that Butworth was murdered for personal motives. Either he was in with some underground operators who wanted him out of the way, or out of revenge for something he did."

"And Snipe had an answer to that? I wouldn't be surprised if he was in with the *Mafiosi*."

"He told me Butworth's murderer lived in this house."

San Angelo frowned. "In this house? How could that be? We have Plymouth on the second floor, a banker of repute. Gregory on the same floor, at the back. A biologist at Columbia. Let's see now, who's on the third? Hawkins. I forget what he does, but he strikes me as a highly respectable man. Harrison on the fourth, of Harrison, Troup and Greene. And in the penthouse, that crippled old lady who gives most of the parties here."

"And Mellon, the janitor."

"A decent chap. He's been here almost as long as I have, and that's nearly twenty years."

"That leaves you," I said.

"Yes," he said, with his usual imperturbability. "That leaves me. Do you think I'd make a good suspect?"

He smiled, that half sarcastic, half sad smile which was so endearing. All I felt then was shame washing over me, shame for having been almost jolted out of my chair when Snipe had mentioned the address. I shook my head.

"Well, your work with the commission will soon be coming to an end, won't it?" said San Angelo. "I understand they were given ten weeks to gather material. Seven have gone by. I'll be glad when you're back in the office again regularly."

"Regularly?" I said. "San, I think I'd still like to have some days off for work I consider more interesting. More necessary," I corrected myself, "than sweating over contracts like this." I pointed to the papers on the desk.

"Tad," he said, "what's got into you? What's so fascinating

about the Butworth case? Other men have been killed. More prominent ones."

And I answered him as I had answered Walter Snipe, "Somehow I feel compelled."

He looked at me long and hard, his pupils contracting. "We shouldn't give in to compulsions. If we did, we could never deal rationally. It's a luxury for which one invariably pays with unhappiness, one's own and that of others. Why do you want to know when Washington doesn't?"

A few hours before I would probably have replied, "Just because of that. The public has a right to know, and the government is withholding that right." Now I didn't know what to say. Snipe had mentioned that a third party was interested in continuing the investigation, but how did I know if I could take Snipe seriously? His conclusions about the house were absurd. There was evidently within me still a deep rejection of occult powers. I remained silent.

Next to San Angelo's front door stood a small table with a drawer. With the upholstered bench opposite, it was the only piece of furniture in the narrow entrance hall. The drawer usually held belongings of the tenants—an extra pair of glasses, a dropped glove, a scarf that had proved unnecessary, things like that. The elevator man collected them, and at some time or other would deliver them to their various owners. He wasn't around right then and I opened the drawer, took all the things in it and stuffed them into my pocket. I would give them to Snipe tomorrow.

CHAPTER

THIRTEEN

I T HAD BECOME A HABIT to call Caroline before I left for
the office, and say good morning to her. She belonged to
that enviable race of people who open their eyes in the
morning and are immediately wide awake and ready to
go. This time it wasn't she who answered but the deep,
pleasant voice of a young man who had slept well, which
I hadn't, and apparently had no problems to face, which
I did.

"Hold it. Caroline's in the bathroom. I'll see if she can
come."

"She'd better," I said, under my breath. I looked at my
watch. It was twenty past eight. What was a man doing in
her studio at this hour? She never started work before nine,
so it couldn't be a client.

"Good morning to you." She sounded slightly muffled. I
knew she washed her hair every day, always under the
shower, and rubbing it dry, the towel sometimes got in the
way.

"Who was that?"

"Per. He just blew in."

"Who is Per?"

"I told you. I went to Greece with him. And he's just

come up with a marvelous proposal. He's going to India and wants me to come along."

"Have fun," I said. It had never occurred to me that Caroline might go off to some other country again. For God knows how long.

"It's going to be fascinating. I've never been to India. Have you?"

"No. But I understand the poverty's pretty depressing, everybody gets a stomach bug, and there's filth all around you."

"Don't encourage me."

"Well, so long, then."

"And don't be so bad-tempered," she said, and it annoyed me that she should be so tactless as to criticize me in the presence of another man. "It's going to take some time to get ready for it. All those injections."

"Yellow fever. Yes," I told her. "Some people have very bad reactions. I knew someone"—no name came to me so I said—"Susy. She got hepatitis and was in the hospital for weeks."

"I'm only allergic to pugnacious people." She hung up, of course. She was quite right. Why should she talk to a bore?

Tiger was a nuisance too that morning. No spot, no tree was to his liking. I had to take him all the way to Washington Square before I could leave for the office. As San Angelo always said, bachelors shouldn't be tied down by animals. They, and babies, belonged under the care of a woman. Susanne had never minded taking Tiger out, but you don't marry a woman to have a dogwalker. Dogwalker, I thought, and was back with Butworth and Percy, the boy whose dog had discovered the body.

My secretary at San Angelo's office—I always thought of it as his—was not a tenth as efficient as Mrs. Johnson, down on Foley Square. She made up for it by being pretty, but prettiness doesn't help one to find a much-needed paper,

and the file clerk was on sick leave. I was invited to have
lunch in the private dining room. It was usually a good
lunch, preceded by drinks, with wine at the table. I didn't
feel like cocktails; in the middle of the day they made me
sleepy. San Angelo fooled everyone by pretending his glass
contained gin instead of Poland water with ice in it. Instead
of joining the men in his office, I called Snipe. Third party.
What had he meant by "a third party" being interested?

"May I come at five?"

He hesitated.

"I've collected quite a few personal items."

"Four would be better if you can make it."

I said yes, I could, and went in to lunch. The usual chit-
chat, some jokes, a few anecdotes, gossip, before coffee was
served and everybody settled down for the real purpose of
the gathering. To anyone else a new oil concession on the
west coast of Africa, and the possibilities of the financial
transactions involved might have been fascinating. To me
they were not. The day dragged on, lightened only by the
appearance of a journalist who had heard something about
the merger of the two companies, which San Angelo and I
had been working on last night, and wondered if I could
give him any information on it. He was obviously a green-
horn who didn't know that lawyers never talked . . . ha-ha
. . . It was a pleasure to tell him to go to hell. Every time I
glanced at the clock on the wall . . . desks had to be as
uncluttered as possible . . . it still seemed to be three. The
damn thing must have stopped. I couldn't stand it any
longer, and left. Again I walked, sneezing frequently, and
not once feeling strange eyes pricking holes in my back.
Instead I thought I could see Caroline and Per on every
street corner, arm in arm, swinging along, shopping for their
trip to India. Idiotic! India had been photographed *ad
nauseam*—thin, rickety cows, beggars breathing their last
on the streets, the Taj Mahal. No publisher would get out
another book on India. If he did, he was a fool.

I reached Fifty-seventh Street and Third Avenue sooner than I had anticipated, but when I tried to enter the house, a policeman stopped me. "Do you live here?"

"No."

"Then what's your business here?"

"I have an appointment."

"With whom?"

"A Mr. Snipe." He was jotting it all down on a little black notebook.

"Your name, please."

I gave it to him, not too happily. I also had to tell him where I lived, and my profession.

"What's all this about? What's wrong?"

He didn't answer and I asked him impatiently if now he would please let me pass.

"I don't know if I can let you pass, sir." He spoke with impressive politeness. "If you'll just wait a moment, I'll get somebody . . ."

He disappeared inside, obviously to ask someone with more authority, and now I noticed a small windowless truck standing at the curb. A medical examiner's bus. When the cop touched my shoulder, I started. "It's okay. You may go up."

There was a policeman in the entrance hall and one on the self-service elevator. "You're a friend of Mr. Snipe?"

"No. I only met him yesterday. Has something happened to him?"

He didn't answer my question right away but proceeded on protocol. "In what respect did you meet him?"

I lied. I told him I intended to become Snipe's patient and that yesterday had been a preliminary interview. "You know how it is, if a doctor's personality doesn't please you . . ."

"Yes, I know." He nodded. "I'm sorry to say that you'll have to look for another doctor. Mr. Snipe is dead."

"But I just talked to him. At twelve. A little after twelve. And he gave me an appointment for four o'clock."

He took that down on a sheet of paper.

"I can't believe it. He looked in perfect health."

The officer shrugged and let me out. There were more people milling around outside the elevator, and quite a few were blocking the entrance to Snipe's apartment. I pushed my way through until I reached a spot from which I could look into the living room. Snipe was hanging by a rope from the wooden curtain rod from which yesterday the monkey had climbed down onto my lap to pat my cheek. A white chalk line had been drawn on the wall-to-wall carpeting and someone had put up a rope about a yard away from the window, to form a square. Inside the rope a man was busy taking fingerprints, another was taking pictures, a third was drawing a map, and a fourth was talking on the telephone.

"Definitely suicide," said a voice behind me, and somebody else, who apparently had some technical knowledge of the various forms death can take, said, "They're not sure yet. It may have been murder. That's why they're going to so much trouble. See, his face is quite pale. Now, when the knot is tied at the side of the neck, the face is often red, because of the total compression of the arteries and veins on that side, but that knot has been tied at the nape of the neck."

"The rope fibers will tell."

"The ambulance guy can't make the decision. That's why they're waiting for the chief."

"I tell you, he was murdered before and strung up later. Look at the position of the body."

"I wouldn't be so sure. You don't need much pressure on the neck. Many hanged persons are found in peculiar positions."

A man stepped forward, obviously a detective. You could tell by the way he was dressed and by his courteousness. "Do all of you people live in this house? If so, please step out. We'll see you later. But if there are any relatives among you, or close friends, would they please remain here."

"I'm a close friend." A tall woman raised her hand. "I took care of him when he had pneumonia two years ago. I sat up with him nights."

"And I cooked for him," said a little girl.

Suddenly there was a commotion at the door. The chief medical examiner had arrived. I squeezed my way, with those who had been asked to leave, out of the apartment and walked down the stairs. Nobody stopped me. Why should they? They had my name and address, and had me down as a prospective patient. I should never have insisted on entering; I should have walked away the moment I'd spotted the windowless truck. Now police would come around to interrogate me. There might even be some publicity. San Angelo would be furious. A member of the firm seeking out a psychologist.

I was shaking so that I didn't realize I was holding onto something, or rather, something was holding onto me. A little black hand had nestled into mine. The monkey.

"Why Mr. Chips! I'm honored that you chose me to help you out. If only you could tell me what happened. Did he kill himself, and why? Or was he murdered? And if he was —why?" I picked him up. He was trembling violently. I put him inside my coat, intending to take him home, then I remembered what Snipe had told me, his partiality to certain colors. Rose had jet-black hair. She wouldn't like to have her face slapped.

I hailed a taxi and drove to Caroline's place. Already from the street I could see that her windows were lit. She took one look at me and brought me a brandy. "Thanks. I needed that." After I had tossed it down, I felt less cold inside.

"What happened? You're white as a sheet."

"Not now. I'll tell you later."

"Here, let me take your coat." I had forgotten to take it off and I wasn't going to take it off now. But then the monkey jumped out from inside it and hugged Caroline, twittering like a bird.

"My God, what's that?"

"A monkey. He loves light hair. His name is Mr. Chips. Your au revoir present."

"You couldn't have found a less practical one?"

"Take care of him for the time being." I turned to go.

"I will," she said, "and call me first chance you get. I'll be in all evening."

After I had left her, I went straight to Manhattan North where I bumped into Lieutenant Jenkins who was on his way out to pick up a bite. He almost fell.

"Easy does it," he said, moving back through the door.

In his office he gave me time to light a cigarette before he asked, "What now? Have you found Butworth's murderer?"

"I would have, if they hadn't killed Snipe before he could tell."

I could have wept. That little man, swinging from a rope, his beautiful face pale, as if in a trance. Jenkins got up and came back with a steaming cup of coffee. "It always straightens me out," he said kindly. "Take all the time you want."

When I was able to speak, he listened intently, without interrupting me. Then he looked up the precinct Fifty-seventh East came under, although I had the feeling he had it at his fingertips and only wanted a few more minutes to think. He dialed a number, asked for a man whose name I didn't catch, gave his, and talked with his hand in front of his mouth so that I could hardly understand what was being said, but when he put the receiver down, he spoke clearly.

"It seems to be homicide all right."

"Maybe somebody knew he kept money in his apartment, or a patient went berserk, or some client to whom he'd given the wrong information . . ." Anything but to have this murder tie up with Butworth's. I was beside myself. If I hadn't sought out his services as a psychic, he might still be alive.

"His rooms were bugged," Jenkins said, and angry suddenly, "I warned you. You can't say I didn't warn you. I told you we didn't want to use a psychic."

"But you didn't tell me why."

"I thought you had enough brains to figure that out for yourself."

So Caroline had been right. They were soft-pedaling the investigation.

I was on the verge of telling him that Snipe had mentioned a third party being interested in the case. I don't know what stopped me, perhaps the picture of Walter Snipe dangling in front of my eyes. Also, I was confused. If Washington didn't consider it desirable to have the truth come out, then where did the third party stand? And had Snipe perhaps been murdered to prevent him from giving me further information?

"How much, exactly, did he tell you about Butworth?"

I hesitated, then lied shamelessly. "All he did was give me an address. The house in which I would find the murderer."

"A respectable house, no doubt. Tenants with impeccable reputations. Well, whoever it is, if he doesn't keep his lip buttoned, he'll end the same way, and that goes for you, my friend. Anyone who has the slightest knowledge about Butworth had better keep it to himself if he wants to stay alive. As far as you are concerned, Mr. Wood, maybe we can kill it."

How poor a thing language is. You used the same word over and over again in so many different ways. Kill. That is—death, the absolute end. In this case kill my being mentioned in any connection with Snipe. "And if not," he said, "since you gave your name—damn your curiosity—you went there to interview him for a friend. What they got by bugging the room, I can take care of. I think."

"I couldn't care less," I said, without regard to whom I was talking, and then, when I saw his face, "what if the place was bugged, not by police but by a different party?"

Jenkins stared at me, then he whistled. I could see he

hadn't thought of such a possibility. He checked himself though, surprisingly fast. "I'll look into it. You go home now, Mr. Wood. Have a drink. Have two. Take a sedative." He grinned. "I do sometimes, and of course those are the nights they call me out of bed."

He came out with me, shook my hand, and strode away. But when I got into a cab that just drew up, I saw him slinking back to his office. I almost got out again to tell him about the monkey, and that Mr. Chips was with Caroline, then thought, what the hell—and gave the driver my address.

CHAPTER

FOURTEEN

I was so tired, I decided not to eat. I did what Jenkins had recommended—had a couple of drinks, later a Nembutal, and had just dropped off to sleep when my doorbell rang. I didn't hear it; Tiger did. I don't know how long he'd been barking; I only knew that something got hold of my leg and shook it.

"Goddamn you," I said, and kicked him away. "I don't want to play with you now." Then the bell rang, very loud and insistent, and I stumbled through the studio and along the passage, cursing and thinking of Jenkins, dragged out of bed when the stuff had just begun to work. I had sense enough to ask who it was before unbolting the door.

"It's me," said a high little voice. "Ellen-Mary."

"Ellen? I don't know any Ellen. Go away, Ellen."

"But you do, Mr. Wood. I'm Melinda's best friend."

Melinda's best friend? She had dozens of best friends. Every boy and girl she met were automatically her best friends. Melinda. When had I heard from her last? I hadn't heard from her at all. Suddenly I was sober. "Come in." And I unlocked the door.

"Thank goodness," said Ellen. "You don't have a doorman, and the buzzer doesn't seem to work, so I waited for simply ages until finally a man came and I got in with him."

"And what brings you here at this unearthly hour?"

"But it isn't an unearthly hour, Mr. Wood. It's early. It's only ten o'clock and the only time I could make it. I told my parents I was going to a movie so they wouldn't expect me home before eleven. I'm only allowed to go to the movies once a week, with friends, of course. So I had to come today."

She looked older than Melinda, maybe a year or two, and she was quite pretty in a cheap way. She had on a minute leather skirt, and a jacket with a long fringe, her hair up and her body loaded with wooden jewelry. Who the hell was she?

"Don't you remember me, Mr. Wood? I'm Ellen-Mary Mellon. My father's the super at Melinda's house."

"Of course. Please forgive me. I remember you, Ellen-Mary. It so happens I was asleep. I'm not usually asleep at this time, so don't feel badly about disturbing me. Now . . . what can I offer you?"

She sat down on the couch. "I really don't want a thing." Remembering her manners, she added, "Thank you."

"Coke? Ginger ale?"

"Would be fine. Unless you happen to have an Irish coffee."

There was some coffee left in the chemex. I heated it up, almost spilling it. I was still pretty groggy. "All I have is bourbon, and no whipped cream, except in a tube."

"That's fine."

She took a sip, shuddered because I had put in too much bourbon, but no protest. She swung one bare leg across the other.

"And now, what can I do for you?"

She sniggered and reached for her handbag, also fringed. "Nothing for me, Mr. Wood, but for Melinda. She's in poor shape. I think she's having a nervous breakdown. Here's a letter for you. She put it in mine." But she didn't hand it to me, a small, square blue envelope. Blue. Melinda's favorite color. "And what a time poor Lindy had, getting it to me. It seems the nuns censor all her mail. She's written to you every day, but she says in the letter to me she's sure you didn't get any of the letters or you'd have acted. Did you get any of the letters?"

"No. I haven't heard from Melinda since she left."

"See?"

"Let me read her letter while you finish your coffee."

"Sure, Mr. Wood. Don't mind me. Come here, Tiger. Remember me? I used to walk you." She grabbed him by the collar. He let her. "He's gorgeous."

And while she was scratching Tiger, I read. "Tad. Come at once. Rescue me, or I'll drown myself in the Tiber. No, not the Tiber, because they won't let me go out alone. Three teachers for ten girls. I can't stand it another minute. If you don't come, I'll tie a cellophane bag around my head after the nuns have checked and the lights are out. I have one, keep it under my pillow. I've tried it already. It's foolproof. I want to live, but not under these circumstances. The doctor says I'm sick and should go to a headshrinker, but I don't want to. Up till now I've been able to resist such idiocy, successfully. I'm not sick. I'm utterly miserable and if that's sick, the only cure for it is to get me away from here fast and back to the States. I'll go to any school San wants to send me to, even if it's not coeducational. Don't tell San about this letter, and don't tell him you're coming. He might stop you. I know you have power of attorney, and you're my godfather, still, you may have to forge his signature, I mean on your request to see me, because he's given strict orders not to let anybody see me. If you can't do that, here's a map, on an extra sheet of paper. We walk that way every day between two and four. Meet me at the place I crossmarked. I love you dearly. And remember, I trust you. You promised to be my friend and now I need a friend. Yours forever, Melinda. P. S. Don't contact my grandmother. She's in cahoots with the nuns and San."

When I looked up from the thin blue paper, Ellen-Mary
was on the floor with Tiger, playing happily with him.
"Ellen," I said, "since when have you and Melinda been
friends?"

"Why, ages. Ever since I can remember. We went to the
same teacher for guitar lessons, and when Lindy took dancing lessons she made San, I mean Mr. San Angelo pay for
mine. In guitar I'm better, but classical dancing is a bore, if
you ask me. Lindy didn't seem to mind practicing at the
barre for hours."

"So you're really close friends."

"Just like sisters. Tell each other everything."

"Did Lindy tell you she didn't want to go to Italy?"

"I'll say she did. She sat in our kitchen and cried for
hours. San beat her something awful."

San Angelo, beating Melinda? The thought was outrageous.

"Why should Mr. San Angelo beat Melinda? He's such a
gentle man, and he adores her."

"He found out."

"Found out what?"

Her face closed like a door on the question. Suddenly her
expression was ridiculously grown up, like that of an adult,
whom life has taught to move with caution.

"Come on," I said. "We're friends, aren't we?" Her lips
tightened in an expression of indecision. "Have you forgotten that I bought you a new bike when yours was stolen,
and you were afraid to go home and tell your parents about
it?"

"I just left it at the bench for a minute."

"But it got pinched."

She sighed. "Yes. And you bought me a new one. I did
appreciate it, Mr. Wood. I always will."

"So?"

"I don't know, Mr. Wood. I don't want to be indiscreet."

"Sometimes we have to be, to help a friend. I thought you
wanted to help Lindy."

"I do want to help her. But will it be helping her if I tell? You're an adult."

"I can't help that."

"I know. You can't help being old."

She finished her coffee. I poured some more bourbon into her empty cup. She laughed. "Did you know she had boy-friends?"

"Of course."

"I warned her. I told her over and over again, Lindy, if I did what you're doing, my father'd kill me if he got wise to it."

"You mean George? Dan? But I think she liked Doug best, don't you?"

Ellen-Mary flopped down on the couch. "Those babies. Who wants green kids? They don't know their front from their rear end. Laurene had one like that and she had to unzip his pants for him and show him how. And they don't know how to kiss. They're all tongue. You have to come up for air when they get going. But Doug's better than the rest."

"How do you know?"

"I inherited him," she said smugly, "when he and Melinda broke up."

I was afraid of saying something that might make her self-conscious. Right now she was enjoying her importance, and the bourbon was beginning to work. I murmured something to the effect that I hadn't known Melinda was already in the necking stage.

"You're kidding. You kissed her. For real."

I hadn't ever kissed Melinda. For real. "She made that up."

"She did? Well, she certainly didn't make up Freddy."

"Freddy?"

"I see you don't know about Freddy."

"I don't. She must have trusted you a lot to tell you about him."

"She did. You see, that's why I feel I shouldn't tell."

"Well, I guess you shouldn't, unless it would help her in some way."

"How do I know you won't use it against her?"

I pretended to be angry. "You know me better than that, Ellen-Mary. Can't you rely on your instincts? Who was Freddy?"

"Any grass around here?" she asked.

Except for a few occasions, I had never smoked pot, but Susanne had. If I was lucky, there might be some in my desk, where she used to hide it from Rose.

"You mean pot," I said slowly. "Now if I were to find some, you could tell on me and I don't know if . . ."

"You know I wouldn't do that, Mr. Wood. Don't be silly."

"All right," I said. "I'll trust you and you trust me."

"Okay," she said.

I got up, went over to my desk, found what Susy had left, two thin joints. I felt pretty awful as I handed them to Ellen-Mary. "Now. Who was Freddy?"

She lit one of the joints. "Freddy," she said, "was her lover."

"Lover? Oh, come on now, Ellen-Mary."

The sweet smell of pot wafted across to me.

"He certainly was. She smuggled him in. Of course I helped her. When the coast was clear, I'd give her a ring on the house phone. That meant either Dad was busy in the basement or the elevator guy was up on the fourth floor, giving Mrs. Abele a hand. She always needed a long time to make it to the elevator on those Canadian crutches. So then Freddy could sneak in. She'd signal him with a flashlight. Two short, one long."

"That doesn't mean he was her lover."

"No? What do you think they did—drink tea? They went straight to your room. Of course only on days when the Rileys were off, Thursday, when Mr. San Angelo works late and usually doesn't come home until midnight. He goes to his club, doesn't he? And plays bridge. Didn't you notice that she didn't go out with you any more Thursday nights?"

It was true. On Thursday, with the Rileys off, San Angelo would stay late at the office, dine out, then go to the club to play cards, and normally I reserved these evenings to take Melinda to a delicatessen and an early movie. But lately— Ellen-Mary was right—Melinda had called me at the last minute to say she was swamped with homework, or had a cold, and couldn't go. Good God, and I had never thought anything of it!

It was just as shocking to imagine Melinda in the arms of a lover as it had been when I had first learned about sex, and had realized that my father and mother were doing what everybody else did, and not only to produce an off-spring, and although I'd gone to a fairly progressive school, with little plaster models in glass cases, showing every detail of the human body, and had them explained to me, still I fought a classmate of mine who had insisted my parents "did it." And Melinda was a child. A twelve-year-old girl.

"But she's much too young for that sort of thing."

Ellen-Mary smiled, the sophisticated smile of older women, out to kill an illusion. "You mean to make love? Oh Mr. Wood . . . I go to a parochial school, and in the basement, where the washrooms are, the boys come in all the time. During recess. Most of them give us the grass for cash, but Bridget's friendly source—and she's only ten—insists on doing it."

"Melinda doesn't smoke pot. I'd have detected it."

"No. She doesn't. She said Freddy was better. She said he was a fun escape from all dreariness."

Tennis, swimming, skating, riding, allowed to bring any friends she wanted to Connecticut; museums, movies, the ballet, every now and then the opera or a theater—how could Melinda see her life as dreary? Was Ellen-Mary transferring the dreariness of her existence to Melinda? Or did a twelve-year-old child—my mind balked at the girl who was ten, besides, it probably wasn't true . . . but did a twelve-year-old child really need sex?

"Did you ever meet Freddy?"

"No," she said, so quickly, I believed her. "He didn't want to meet anyone. Naturally. After all . . ."

"What's his last name?"

She hesitated, then asked if it would be all right if she smoked the second joint. I struck a match and lit it for her. She liked that. "I don't know," she said. "But I know what he looks like. I caught a glimpse of him once. Good looking. But old. I asked her, can he still perform? She said, like a breeze. He has a beard and a mustache. Some girls like the way they tickle. Maybe that's why so many boys have them now, not because they stand for protest." She giggled. "Wouldn't that be a scream? Personally I prefer a clean-shaven face like yours, Mr. Wood." She inhaled deeply. "And he spoiled her rotten. Presents, presents . . ."

"What kind of presents?"

"Want a drag?" She held out the cigarette, watching me out of the corners of her eyes. I accepted the short, lipstick-smeared stub, then carefully passed it back to her. She had a little gadget to pick it up, so as not to waste any. She looked more relaxed. Now she could say we'd smoked pot together, and that I'd furnished it. To a minor. "What kind of presents?"

"The best," she said. "Money. What can you do with anything else? Your parents spot it as soon as it's in your room. But money . . ." Her nose crinkled up. "That's a girl's best friend. You can take a taxi instead of the subway, go to a movie and invite the whole gang, and of course get all the hash you want. Melinda was always very generous. She gave me half, at least that's what she said. Twenty-five bucks every Friday. That's a lot when two dollars pocket money is all you have."

"It certainly is, Mary-Ellen."

"It's Ellen-Mary."

"Sorry. Ellen-Mary, have you told anybody what you've just told me?"

"I'm not an informer."

"I wasn't suggesting you are."

"Cross my heart," and she drew a cross with her chubby forefinger between her already quite heavy breasts. "I only told you because Melinda needs you. I haven't talked to another soul and I don't intend to."

I thought of offering her money to keep her mouth shut, but I didn't want her to think it was all that important whether she talked or not. "That's good," I said. "A true friend keeps secrets, and I see now you're Lindy's true friend."

"I sure am."

"If you breathe a word, Lindy could never come back. If it came out, no decent school would accept her. So just forget all about it, right?"

"And you forget about me, Mr. Wood. My dad'd kill me if he knew I'd helped her let Freddy in. He thinks nothing goes on in that house he doesn't know about. He's so proud of it, poor guy."

"And now let me put you in a cab. It's ten minutes past eleven. We don't want your parents worrying about you."

After she'd gone I made myself some strong coffee. Then I called the airlines. There was no plane, next day, directly to Rome, but TWA had one going to London around nine, with a connection to Rome a half hour later. I booked on it. Then I dialed Jenkins' number. He had given it to me before I left him. "It's okay if I leave the country for a few days?"

"I wish you'd stay out of it altogether."

Then I phoned Mrs. Johnson. "I just want you to know that I won't be in the office tomorrow, maybe not on Thursday either."

"Where are you off to?"

"To bed. I have a beaut of a cold." I coughed and spoke nasally. "And I'm not taking any calls. I'm sure you can handle everything that may come up."

"I'll do my best," she said pleasantly. "Let me know if there's anything I can do."

I got Mrs. Riley on the phone, which was a piece of luck. San Angelo would have wanted to know where I was going.

"Yes, Mr. Tad?"

"Tell Mr. San Angelo I'll have to go out of town for a couple of days, maybe longer."

"So you won't be coming to Ridgefield with us?"

"Can't. My loss. Just be sure you don't forget to tell him in the morning."

"You know I never forget anything."

And finally I called Caroline. I started off casually. "How are your plans progressing?"

"Per isn't sure yet. It may be Hong Kong instead of Calcutta, or it may be Australia. He's itching to go somewhere that isn't the Western Hemisphere, but he's got to talk to publishers first." She didn't comment on the fact that it was after midnight and I should have known that by this time she was in bed. For a young woman she had a rigid routine —up at seven, an hour's walk, breakfast at eight, shower at eight thirty, start work at nine. If possible, see no customers before eleven. An hour's rest between one and two. Stop work at five. Clean the studio, have a drink, dinner, work again or go to a play or a movie. Exceptions only when she thought it necessary. And she clung to this schedule as someone drowning might cling to a lifebelt. Until she became my wife, I didn't stand a chance of changing her way of life. "How's the monkey?"

"Fine. He's sleeping next to me in a crib I bought for him. But even the pet store wasn't sure what to feed him. I'm terribly uneducated when it comes to monkeys. I don't know what to give him. He seems to like bananas and milk. I had the milk tepid, thought that was safest. You see, I'm trying to walk the golden middle way."

"Call the Bronx Zoo. They'll advise you."

"Where did you get him, and why?"

"I'll tell you when I get back."

"Going somewhere?"

"Abroad."

"Really?"

"Something came up unexpectedly."

"When will you be back? Or don't you know?"

"In a couple of days at the most. And will you take care of Tiger?"

"Of course," she said. "I always wanted a menagerie."

"I want to make a date with you, for the weekend."

"The weekend's taken."

"By Per?"

"Yes."

"Next Monday then."

"Wonderful."

"And Caroline, listen to me . . . what are you doing? You sound so far away suddenly."

"I've got a corn on my little toe. I was picking it."

The last time I had seen her, her feet had been flawless. I thought she was lying. Maybe Per was lying beside her and had caused her to move away from the receiver. "Don't pick at it," I told her, trying to keep my voice casual. "And listen to me. Are you listening? Okay. Now . . . if you still have anything, anything at all that belonged to your father, destroy it. Burn it. At once."

There was a stillness over the wire that frightened me. "Caroline, are you still there?"

"I told you I have nothing."

"What about the notebook one of the detectives tried to pinch?"

"I told you I burned everything."

I couldn't tell her about Snipe, I couldn't mention Jenkins, and least of all could I convey to her the dreadful thoughts about her father that were beginning to take shape in my mind after my talk with Ellen-Mary. All I could say was, "Caroline, I can't help feeling that you're holding something back, that there's still something in your apartment, and I'm trying to tell you that it's dangerous to keep anything. So burn it. Now! Do you hear me?"

"Over," she said, still trying to make a joke of it.

"I want to see you again when I get back."

"Oh, but you will."

"I mean, *alive*," and I hung up for greater emphasis. It took all my willpower.

CHAPTER

FIFTEEN

S AN ANGELO ALWAYS FLEW FIRST CLASS. I could afford it, but felt somehow that it was unbecoming for an able-bodied young man to indulge in such luxury. This morning, though, I cursed the frugal trait which I must have inherited from my father's family. The plane was crowded, I was seated between two women, each with a scent that was cheap and penetrating. They were short two stewardesses, and it took a long time until I was served. Not that I was hungry. I was just being difficult. I had a right to be fed so I asserted my rights.

We were flying through the clouds, and much as I'd enjoyed, as a child, seeing strange shapes and pictures in their formations, I turned my head away. Now they held nightmare images—Melinda in bed with an elderly man, a man with a beard. Why had I forgotten to ask Ellen-Mary what kind of a beard he was wearing? Surely she had made up most of it. At thirteen, fourteen, you made up things. I had. I had told Justo, long before I'd ever come close to a girl, that she'd kissed me passionately. At that age you have fantasies; reality never suffices. Melinda had shown off and Ellen-Mary had exaggerated.

I couldn't concentrate on reading. I had bought several

papers at the airport. Most of them showed Snipe dangling from the curtain rod, the way I had seen him last. One paper even mentioned that he had owned a monkey, and that the monkey had disappeared. Well, there surely were hundreds of Capuchins in New York. Nobody could connect Caroline with Snipe.

Snipe. He wouldn't stop dangling before my eyes. When I'd told him I'd see him soon, he had replied, "I don't think so." Had he known he would die before I got to him with the odds and ends I had collected? Of course not. He had made an appointment with me for four o'clock, made it shortly after noon. And between noon and four he had been killed.

And there was San Angelo. Beating Melinda. I couldn't believe it. Whatever he'd found out. The man didn't have it in him. Or did he? He was an Italian. Italians were hot-headed. But he was also controlled, one of the most con-trolled men I had ever known. Not the innate control that is handed down through generations, which I knew my father had possessed to a high degree, and to some extent, I hoped, was present in me, but an educated control, ingrained by learning and by my father's influence. The most reliable kind. It was preposterous, all of it, and all of it put into my mind by a little show-off who wanted an Irish coffee, about which she must have heard somehow or other, that it was the *non plus ultra*. Pot, sex, and Irish coffee. And Caroline? She was in danger. She knew something about her father that other people either wanted her to tell or keep quiet. I refused to guess what.

Finally—Heathrow. Fogged in. And the long walk to the lobby. And a delay on the plane to Rome.

In Rome my mood changed. I felt less depressed. But then I had always loved Rome. Not only because I'd been there at an age when history came to life for one, or because it had been fun to fold little paper boats and watch them sail across the Fontana Trevi to the Goddess of Fertility, or because Justo had still been alive, and we had met Clarissa. At the Ponte Sant' Angelo. Justo had stopped her and said, "This bridge belongs to my family. I am a San Angelo."

I had no desire to contact Melinda's grandmother, even without Melinda's warning. I'd met Mrs. Bongrani when Clarissa had invited us to tea at her mother's house. Already then she had been a widow, one of those women whose husband's duty it is to die early and leave a lot of money while they are still young enough to enjoy it. Maybe she had changed, maybe she had let the Titian red dye grow out of her hair and was now a gray-haired old lady, acting her age, but I preferred not to risk it. However, just to play it safe, so that nobody could say later that I'd gone to Italy only to see Melinda, I called up a client Lorenzo Cotti and was lucky enough to find he could see me any time. I made an appointment with him for dinner.

I rented a car at the airport, a small Fiat, and drove off. There was more traffic than I remembered from my last visit, a couple of years ago, more noise, more American tourists, more people who dressed like Americans, more drugstores and hamburger stands at corners that had been happily free of such enterprises. But the smell was the same—strong coffee, manure, and flowers. And the bells rang out just as loudly and measuredly as they always had. Little children were still elegantly dressed and being taken care of by nannies in smart uniforms. The old women hadn't yet discarded their dirty, black wool scarves, which they wore around head and shoulders, and flower girls still crossed against the light to offer you carnations, mimosa, and violets on straw trays. I bought three bunches of violets, because I'd brought nothing for Melinda, and was cheated of about thirty-five cents, but my Italian had become too rusty to argue, besides, the girl was pretty. I stopped later at a confectioner's shop to get some blanched almonds and half a pound of candied violet leaves. I ate most of the almonds myself, out of the expensive little bag, tied with three different colored

ribbons, as I drove up the narrow, winding, tree-studded
road of one of Rome's seven hills, the Monte Pincio, and on
to the Parioli district where modern apartment houses stood
side by side with private villas, some still hidden behind
their high walls, above which only the tops of trees could be
seen, and now and then, through a wrought-iron gate, a
piece of carefully tended lawn or flower beds. In one of
those houses we had flirted with Melinda's mother under
the stern glance of her governess.

Unexpectedly a sign warned of a school crossing, and
there it was, the Convent School Santa Veronica. A thin bell
tolled the hour. It didn't look at all forbidding, but I could
understand that for Melinda it had to be a prison. She
hated to be fenced in; even in Connecticut she resented the
low stone walls everyone else found so charming. "All sorts
of creepy crawlies live in them. I hate snakes, and I don't
like lizards either. And anyway, they're an obstacle."

There would be no snakes or reptiles in these smooth
walls, but they were certainly high. There was a wide gate
opening out on a parking lot with an attendant, and a
smaller one with an electric button set in the brick. A sister
appeared almost as soon as I rang. My arrival must have
been observed from inside. I handed her the letter I had
typed last night, "To whom it may concern." Melinda had
failed to give me the name of the mother superior, and
rather than make a mistake, I had kept the tone general.
"This is to introduce Melinda's godfather, Mr. Thaddeus J.
Wood. I would appreciate it if you would let Melinda spend
some time with him." And then I had forged his signature.
San Angelo. And added the address and telephone number.

"Follow me, please."

I was led into a reception room. Its modern furniture almost made me gasp. No blown-up chairs, but chrome and
leather ones that looked incongruous on the old mosaic
floor. An older nun came through a narrow door, held open

by the same young nun who had let me in. "I'm Sister Agatha. Delighted to meet you, Mr. Wood." She was very good looking and I wondered what she would be like without her wimple and her long, dark skirt. Since she kept her arms folded below her breasts, I didn't offer my hand but merely bowed. "Sister Agatha, I am here only for a day, and maybe a few hours tomorrow. If you could possibly arrange for me to see my godchild, I would be very grateful."

"Melinda is at prayers."

"I'll wait, if you don't mind."

"Mr. San Angelo didn't announce your coming."

"He thought the letter would be sufficient. I left rather unexpectedly. If you have any doubts, why don't we phone him?"

The shadow of a smile crossed her face. "I'm afraid our phone service isn't quite up to what you're accustomed to. It would take hours."

"I'm allowed to wait then?"

"Is it true that you can dial the continent directly from America?"

"From some places, yes."

"I understand you are a partner of Signore San Angelo. I studied law, and I am still working as a lawyer, although part of my time is taken up with teaching English."

Hers was perfect. "Church law? I'm afraid I'm not very familiar with it."

"A complicated subject, and not easy in our times. Sometimes I think of that old prophecy of the pilgrims who visited the Colosseum. 'While stands the Colosseum, Rome shall stand; when falls the Colosseum, Rome shall fall; when Rome falls, with it shall fall the world.' The Colosseum has always been a symbol."

"And it still stands."

"Some ruins, yes. But can we protect them from complete destruction? With the air poisoned and the great noise and dreadful vibrations all around them nowadays?" She looked up. "Melinda, I am sorry to say, is not devout. She lacks . . ."

"I'm afraid she wasn't brought up to consider religion very important."

"But Signore Angelo must be religious. He has just given us a very generous sum."

I couldn't very well tell her that I didn't know how deeply felt was San Angelo's faith, but that my guess was he'd rather spend some money than participate actively as a church member.

"How is Melinda doing otherwise?"

"It is not her ability to learn that worries me." Sister Agatha sighed. "She's bright, perhaps too bright. It's her attitude. Other children are obstreperous, even belligerent, but with her it takes the form of open rebellion. She is not a good influence on her classmates. She is always putting them up to something, pranks, sometimes worse than pranks."

"For instance?"

"She has an inflated ego, and she expects everybody to see things her way. She won't obey rules; she'd rather be punished. She doesn't seem to understand that only by submission, by putting aside one's personal desires and becoming a link in the chain can she achieve peace and satisfaction and become a true servant of God. She isn't willing to serve. Life has to serve her."

"But Sister Agatha, Melinda isn't going to become a nun."

"A pity. We need bright young creatures, we need girls who are full of life. If it can be channeled in the right direction. With Melinda I fear that is impossible. She doesn't realize, she doesn't want to realize that only as part of a community can we survive."

"I'll talk to her about it."

"I wish you would."

Somewhere a bell tolled. Sister Agatha turned to the younger sister who hadn't moved from her place at the door. "Be good enough, Sister Sabrina, to have Melinda San Angelo called."

A few minutes later Melinda came into the reception room. She was dressed in a black school uniform which made her look very pale. Her hair was braided in one long braid, but otherwise combed out of her face, which laid bare the perfect lines of its bone structure more clearly than before, but also made her look older.

"You may have half an hour with your godfather."

Melinda curtsied. "And may we walk out into the garden? It's so stuffy in here. And I couldn't take part in the exercises today because I had a headache."

"You may. Good-bye, Mr. Wood. If you do stay over to-morrow, I would very much like to talk to you at length."

"A pleasure."

As soon as Sister Agatha had gone, Melinda whispered, "Turn left and left again, and we'll be in the garden."

"Why the garden? It's chilly out now."

"I'm sure they have this place bugged. Come on."

She hadn't touched my hand or embraced me, but once in the garden, after a careful look over her shoulder, she held me tight. "Thank you for coming, Tad. I knew you would. Thank God you did."

We walked along a brick path under low arches to a mar-ble bench at the far end of the small garden. As soon as we had sat down, I said, "Lindy, I don't have much time, and if you're not willing to tell me the full truth, I won't help you to get back to the States. We've only got half an hour, so don't let's waste it. I talked to your friend Ellen-Mary last night, so I know a lot more than you may think."

She was cagey. "What did she tell you?"

"About Freddy and how you used to smuggle him into the apartment."

"Only a few times, and I was a goddamn fool to do it. If we'd just gone to the usual place, no one would have found out."

"What's Freddy's last name?"

"I don't know. 'Just call me Freddy,' he said."

"Where did you meet him?"

"In the park."

"And he asked you straight away if . . . if you and he . . ."

"No, no. We were lying on the grass."

"When?"

"I just told you. In the park. Ellen-Mary and I went to a rock concert. We said our teacher was taking a bunch of us. And we couldn't get tickets. But it's much better outside anyway—no narrow chairs, you can stretch out. Ellen-Mary had brought along a blanket. In an interval I got up to buy some ice cream. They come down there with their wagons. And there was Freddy, and he offered to pay. And why not? Gentlemen treat ladies, don't they? I brought Ellen-Mary her cone, and then looked for him. He was still there. He had a blanket too. And I stretched out next to him. Ellen-Mary was mad. She couldn't find anyone. There were mostly groups, no single boys, so she went home in a huff."

"But you stayed."

"The concert wasn't over."

"And what did he say?"

"You sound like a cop."

"Never mind. What did he say?"

"He didn't say anything."

"Melinda, if you won't talk, we're not going to get anywhere."

"He put his hand between my legs. No, first on my breasts."

"And?"

"It felt good."

"You made love?"

"Are you crazy? With no second blanket to cover us, and patrolmen on the rocks?"

"But you did make love. Eventually."

"And why not?"

"I could think of a few reasons. A kid, twelve years old."

"There are tribes where girls are mothers at ten."

"That doesn't apply. Why did you do it?"

"Because I felt like it. Because he made me feel like it. Because he was sweet."

"Where did you make love?"

"At his place."

"And where was that?"

"I promised not to tell. Oh, Tad, I miss him like hell."

"Have you any idea how old he was?"

"Ancient," said Melinda. "San's age, I'd say. Maybe older. What has age got to do with sex? I think San would be much better off if he had a young girl who could make him forget how old he was."

"Not that young. Where did he take you?"

"You won't give up, will you?"

"No. I want to know."

"But you must promise not to tell anyone. Or go there."

"I promise."

"It was a studio, downtown. He was a photographer. And he took pictures of me."

"You mean you posed for him?"

"Sometimes of me alone, sometimes the two of us together. It's quite easy to take a picture of yourself if you rig up the camera correctly and get a wire to where you're lying and press the button once you're in the right position."

"Weren't you ashamed?"

"Of what? I've got a lovely body. Are those violets for me?"

"Yes. I bought them for you."

"You wasted your money. We're not allowed to have flowers in our rooms. All of them go to the chapel or hospitals. May I have one of the candies? You didn't offer me one and you've been munching them all the time."

"Here." I passed her the bag. "Do you have any of those pictures?"

She had stuffed so many of the candied violet leaves in her mouth, she had to swallow before she could answer. "Just one. Of him. A good one. It's in my hot water bottle bag. I cut it open, shoved the picture in, then glued it together again. But I have a whole film roll. He never let me have them, but I managed to pinch this one. It isn't developed yet. There wasn't time."

"I want that roll of film, and I want the picture."

"I don't know how to get them to you. If I go in now, I have to ask permission to come out again. Well, maybe it can be done. I'll think of a way. Tad, what are you looking at me that way for? What's so horrible about having had sex? Keeps the world going, he said, and it does, Tad. It does. Don't look at me that way. After all, I haven't killed anyone."

That brought me out of my stupor and to the point of my coming here. "Lindy, what happened the night San discovered you and whipped you?"

"San never whipped me. He spat at me."

"I want to know exactly what happened."

"Don't shout."

"I wasn't shouting. Sorry."

"It was just one of those things. A Thursday. That was the only day I could have Freddy up. He called, at six as usual and I said I was too tired to come downtown."

"It was a long way?"

She fell for it. "Nineteenth Street. You have to take a bus, then the subway. So I told him to come up. The Rileys were out, San was playing bridge, the usual setup. He'd called home earlier to see if I was all right and not to worry if he was late and to phone him at the club if I felt lonely. Ellen-Mary was watching out for me, so I thought I was safe. Anyway, I always used your room, I knew you wouldn't mind, because if I heard the front door opening, he could slip down to the kitchen and out the back entrance before anyone could come up to the first floor. But San quite unexpectedly had changed his mind about playing bridge and came home at a time I could not possibly have thought he would. Before eight o'clock, I think. He must have opened the door so carefully, I didn't hear a thing. Neither did Freddy, and he always had one ear cocked like a fox. You know, the one that comes up to the swimming pool. He always cocks one ear. I know San didn't mean to spy on me. That's something he's never done. He just didn't want to wake me. But you know how he has this infantile habit of looking in on me to see if I'm asleep, and tuck me in like a baby."

"Stop eating those candies or you'll be sick. So what happened?"

"He must have tiptoed up the stairs and to my room, and when he didn't find me in bed, walked on until he saw the light under the door of your room. And he opened the door and saw us."

"And then?"

"Well, I never saw anyone dress so fast. And he never called me again."

"I mean San. What did he do?"

"He just stood there like someone frozen to the ground. And then he said, 'Get out before I kill you,' and closed the door. And Freddy got out, without kissing me good-bye, and after a little while San came back—I was still in your room—and spat at me. Just spat at me. He didn't say anything. But next morning he told me that he didn't want to see me for a while, maybe never again, and that he would send me away, and all that crap about being rotten through and through, and that I must never mention what had gone on between Freddy and me to anyone or he'd die of shame, or wring my neck, or both. Things like that. And then he started blaming himself and finally, can you imagine it, he cried! He put his hands in front of his face but the tears trickled through his fingers, right onto his scrambled eggs. And then I felt awful."

I found I couldn't speak, and Melinda sat quietly too, holding herself strangely upright, like someone exhausted but determined not to show it. "Melinda," I said finally, "did you ever tell anyone about all this?"

"Never. I swear I didn't. All Ellen-Mary knows is that Freddy came to visit me secretly."

"You didn't boast about it to any of your boyfriends?"

She shook her head. "I told you, I didn't talk about it to anyone. Tad, there are no virgins anymore, except for the Virgin Mary, and she's just a symbol. It still stands, doesn't it? That if you're not married by the time I'm sixteen and I still feel about you the way I do now . . ."

"You didn't feel the same way when you allowed Freddy to make love to you."

"Don't be silly," she said. "That's just what woke me up to how I feel about you. Every time I'd been with him, I'd think of you that way. I didn't love him. I love only you. But you'd never have done it with me. You're too much of a square. You measure that sort of thing by age and God knows what else. And now that I've told you everything, the truth, the whole truth and nothing but the truth, what are you going to do for me to get me out of here?"

"I want you to give me his picture and the roll of film."

She screwed up her face. "That's not going to be easy." And then, "Oh, I know what I'll do. I'll ask Sister Agatha for permission to give you some pictures I've taken, for my grandfather."

"And then I want you to go to that psychiatrist you wrote me about."

"Oh God, must I? I can't stand it here any longer. Don't you understand?" Her eyes were full of tears. "Can't you take me with you? Now?"

"I wish I could," I said. "And I promise I'll help you. I have some very nice young friends in Switzerland. Maybe they'll have you. But it may take a little while."

"Don't let it take too long," said Melinda. "Hurry, before I do something really silly."

CHAPTER

SIXTEEN

U NLESS YOU SLEEP AT NIGHT, you become a victim of its power. The power of darkness, that knows no limitations, no height, no depth. There is a quality to its black magic that intensifies beauty as well as horror. You hear a child cry, and it is the cry of all children. Or laughter, and the laughter is all around you, a never-ending echo. Its sadness is bottomless, its joy reaches the sky. And in the fear of its darkness, the agony of all humans is exaggerated to a point that reaches insanity.

Although I had given the roll of film and the photo of Butworth to Cotti over dinner, and asked him to please mail them to me, air mail, insured, at the Fifth Avenue address, I could find no rest. I tossed from side to side. I longed for a spot of coolness on my pillow where I could lay my burning forehead. I imagined woods, and at once trees grew around me, enormously tall, a solid wall, a prison I couldn't escape. Somewhere this forest had to end. But it didn't. I searched for a way out, knowing I was trapped, and the surer my knowledge that I would never see open country again, the more desperate I became. I thought, a boy catches a fish and is happy to have caught it. He cleans it, cooks it, eats it. He isn't aware that he has just killed a living creature. For him it's sport. A twelve year old is hungry for sex, so she satisfies her hunger. From her point of view it happens to be natural. They say a boy becomes a man when he catches his first fish, and nobody finds anything wrong with it. On the contrary, he is congratulated and he is proud. The act signals a coming of age. "It felt good," Melinda had said, and with the act had become a woman. Why was the one acceptable and not the other? Morals were an invention, a device to safeguard yourself and others. Melinda apparently had no conception much less use for the device. "Tut, tut, child," said the Duchess. "Everything's got a moral if only you can find it." Who had? Perhaps Oscar Wilde was right when he wrote that morality was simply the attitude we adopt toward people whom we personally dislike. I couldn't dislike Melinda.

Again and again I turned on the light on my bedside table, but dark or light I could not dispel Butworth's face, with wig and beard, as depicted on the photo Melinda had given me. None of the pictures the police photographer had taken on the spot in Central Park had ever been published in any papers or magazines, nor had I seen them. I had asked Momford to get them to me after I'd gone through Butworth's hate mail. So far he hadn't done so. I had never realized what a wig, a beard, and a mustache could do to a man's face to transform it. It would have been impossible for anyone, even someone who knew Butworth relatively well, to recognize him. Certainly not San Angelo.

I had looked at the picture too long. Now I couldn't escape it—a good face, a gentle face, a face you could trust. Lean features, thoughtful eyes. An elderly man. "Ancient," according to Melinda. And how devastated he must have been to be discovered. Had he thought of death then? Or that he deserved it? And I could see him walking into Cen·tral Park, see San Angelo rushing at him with a knife. San Angelo. I couldn't believe it. San Angelo was no killer.

But when does a man become a killer? Melinda had been his treasure, all that was left of his son Justo. And he had hoped for a large family, a bevy of grandchildren. And Melinda, a child to him, a child with no sexual desires, deflowered. He would see it that way. He was an old-fashioned man for whom the virtue of women was sacred. And who else could possibly have had a motive?

Dawn is a merciful thing. With its first gray light it begins to interfere with the power of darkness, dispelling it softly, gradually. Things begin to show up for what they are—a bench, a single tree, a building. They come into view slowly yet forcefully, one after the other. You begin to see the skyline of a city, a church spire isn't a mile high monster anymore. There are no wild animals in the trees, just a car driving between them, its headlights paled by the dawn, no longer as penetratingly bright as the eyes of an evil spirit. The shadows in which unknown dangers lurked, disappear, one after the other. There is a road, a house, more houses, some windows already lit in kitchens and bathrooms. Behind them people, moving around, getting ready for a new day. The man you have known all your life again becomes the person you loved and respected; the girl you want to marry, innocent; a child is a child again. You had a nightmare, and in a nightmare anything can happen. Hell withdraws before the rising sun. But Justice Butworth's face remained with me, and Melinda's voice saying, "I felt like it. He made me feel like it."

CHAPTER

SEVENTEEN

O^{F ALL THE BUILDINGS AT KENNEDY, TWA is, I think,} the best to arrive at. Its jet-age architecture lends it beauty as well as majesty on a human scale. Furthermore, it's clean. There are enough ashtrays and litter baskets, and plenty of employees sweeping the smooth red carpet and picking up bottles and newspapers carelessly left behind by passengers. I took the escalator down, passed through customs, gave my luggage to a man who put it on the carrier, went through the gate where nobody was waiting to greet me, down another escalator and picked up my single bag from one of the turn tables. Waving a porter away, I crossed the roads, swarming with buses, taxis, private cars, to the parking lot where I had left my Buick. Two nights and a day ago.

It was farther away than I remembered, a three-year-old model that had never given me any trouble. This time the lock of the door did. Needs some oil, I thought, or maybe it's frozen, and I bumped against it to loosen the mechanism. And then it happened. Three men loomed up out of the dark and formed a semicircle around me, with my back to the car. Up to now I'd been one of the lucky few who had never been mugged, so I didn't at first recognize the sudden hollow

feeling in my stomach as fear. I'd taken some judo lessons
the year before, but my reflexes seemed paralyzed. My
brain, though, worked, to a degree. It kept sending me
messages, like someone ticking out the text of a cable. If
you can't protect yourself, give in. If you have a chance,
fight. Fight with your teeth, your nails, shove your fist into
the aggressor's mouth, kick his groin, and scream. Scream
as loud as you can. It may frighten the aggressor away. But
I couldn't scream. Perhaps the realization that nobody would
hear throttled me. Also, there was not just one aggressor,
there were three. It wouldn't do me any good to fight. I had
only one mouth to bite, two hands to hold them off with
and one leg to stand on if I kicked one of the three. They
didn't move. They just stood there, their faces unrecogniz-
able in the dark, their hands in their pockets, in complete
silence. And it was their silence that chilled me. If they
were out to kill me, I didn't stand a chance.

I went down the moment a fist struck my chin. Maybe it
was the coward's way out, but I didn't care much about
being roughed up. One man grabbed my bag. He put it on
the hood of my car, and as if he had nothing to fear, went
through its contents with a flashlight. The second man knelt
beside me on the ground, the third stood over me, but now
he had one hand out of his pocket. He was holding a gun. I
lay motionless while my pockets were being searched, every
one of them, quietly, quickly, efficiently. The man took
everything I owned, even unfastened the watch from my
wrist. Then all of a sudden they were gone, become one
with the night. I told myself to wait, to lie still, and I did,
for a few minutes. Then I got up. My nose was bleeding, so
was a cut on my lip. I leaned against my car until I felt I
could walk back across the lot to the attendant. He wasn't
interested. "Happens all the time. We should have more
lights and more men around." He loaned me his flashlight.
I found my wallet, which they had discarded. It was
empty. The keys to my apartment were gone, but the keys

to the car were still stuck in the lock. Had somebody tampered with the car? I decided not to use it. "I'll pick it up tomorrow," I told the attendant, "or somebody will. But my ticket's gone."

He made me out a new one.

A bus seemed safer than a taxi. I had to wait quite a while for one, and by the time I got into it, it was crowded. Most of the arrivals from my plane had left long ago. I slumped down in the seat behind the driver and he turned around. "Care for an aspirin, Mister? I always carry them with me."

"And here's a Kleenex," said a woman across the aisle. "Or maybe you'd prefer one of these," and she pulled out of her bag a small envelope, the kind you're given on trains and planes after a meal. "One of the few innovations I really enjoy." I could imagine her swiping a handful.

I took the aspirin and the wash'n'dry. I'd been a fool not to go back to the TWA building and clean up before taking the bus. Now their rare human kindliness forced me to reveal that I'd been mugged, and the driver told of his experiences and the woman told of hers, and other passengers chimed in, all agreeing that I'd been lucky to get away without murder. Then they went on to discuss the rising crime rate, while all I could think of was—who had known that I was returning on a certain plane? Who, for that matter, could have known that I'd gone to Italy? And seen Melinda? And got the proof I was after? Thank God I hadn't been carrying the photo and films on me, but had given them to Cotti to mail.

I had to wake the superintendent to let me in, and listen to his commiserations before I could tell him to have the lock on my door changed first thing in the morning. I had forgotten that I had asked Caroline to take care of Tiger. Without him and his joyous bark, the apartment seemed empty and a good deal less safe. I walked through the kitchen, bathroom, living room, making sure no one was lurking anywhere or had tampered with any locks on doors or drawers. Before I went upstairs, I took my revolver out of my desk drawer. I counted the bullets in the carton. All twenty-four were still there. I took six, loaded the gun, and opened the door to the bedroom. It was exactly as I had left it. Only a note was stuck on my pillow, in Rose's sprawling handwriting. "You owe me three dollars and forty-three cents. Have bill. I took milk and butter home, and four eggs. No point wasting food."

I thought of calling Momford, but decided it would be better to contact Jenkins. I asked him to have one of his men get my car, but to make sure first that there was nothing wrong with it.

"Where did you go? I mean, where have you come back from?"

"Italy," I told him.

"Thought you might have gone to Switzerland to look into one of those bank accounts people are keeping there nowadays."

"Not only nowadays," I said, "but ever since the Swiss decided to hang onto their neutrality. Nice people, the Swiss. But Wood, San Angelo and Benson don't handle clients who have no faith in the U.S. currency."

"What did you do in Italy?"

"I went to see a girlfriend."

"Three thousand miles there and back? I'm afraid that lowers my estimation of you. I only have to go around the corner for a good lay."

"You're lucky," I said, and hung up. Then I called Caroline. I could hear Tiger bark when she lifted the receiver. He always barked when a bell sounded. An annoying habit.

"I was afraid you might have left already."

"How could I? I would have found a kennel for your dog, but monkeys are difficult to board."

"I'd like to cancel our date on Monday. All right with you if we change it to Tuesday?"

She was leafing through pages in her diary or calendar; the thin penetrating noise of leaves being turned was audible. "Don't tell me you can't make it. It's important that I see you as soon as possible."

"Then we'll make it Tuesday. Thank you for letting me know you're back."

Good manners are laudable; besides, they make it easier to get along, but right now I couldn't have cared less about politeness.

CHAPTER

EIGHTEEN

"I MISSED YOU THIS WEEKEND," said San Angelo. He was setting up the chessboard. "Without Melinda and you, Laughing Echo wasn't the same place. Besides, it was cold. You could hardly walk, it was so icy."

"Mind if I get myself some Scotch?"

"Go ahead."

"May I fix you something?"

"I'd rather stick with the wine. Mixing drinks hasn't agreed with me lately. What happened to your lip?"

"One of my judo lessons. A brown shirt made a wrong move. I had it sewed up this morning."

"Looks all right now."

"I guess it is."

I went over to the bar again, a small folding table with glasses and ice on top, bottles underneath on the second tray. "Take it easy," said San Angelo. "You look done in. And you had three gins before dinner, and wine, and now . . ."

I came back to the chessboard, full glass in hand, and sat down opposite him. The board was a present I'd given him years ago, a good one, with the men carved in ivory, delicate but slightly yellowed.

"Your move." San Angelo picked a cigar from a box. Havanas were still being mailed to him by friends, two or three at a time. "Last time I started." He bit off a piece of tobacco and put it in a silver ashtray. I watched the match he had forgotten to blow out curl into a wrinkled black worm. I put my drink down on the side table. I said, "You killed Justice Butworth."

The accusation stood in the room like something that had taken on human shape. A stranger, whose face neither of us could see.

San Angelo didn't seem aware of him. "Your move," he repeated, as if I had said nothing.

God only knew what effort it had taken to formulate what I wanted to say, how many hours I had paced up and down, trying to phrase the thing correctly. I hadn't intended it to come out that abruptly. I'd planned to lead up to it gradually. Now I was stunned by my audacity, which was so obviously being ignored by him. "San," I said, "you stabbed Butworth to death."

"I heard you."

"And?"

"And it's the height of nonsense, even for you."

"I knew you'd deny it."

"Did you?"

"You were the one who taught me to deny all accusations. First rule—deny; second rule—keep on denying; third rule —deny until you know it's useless." The stranger in the room moved slowly. He put an invisible hand on my shoulder, as if he wanted to warn me not to raise my voice. "It won't get you anywhere," I said.

"Suppose I did it," he said, blowing a cloud of smoke directly into my face, then waving the cloud away. "Sorry. Would you dare sit in judgment over me, Tad?" He pronounced my name the way he had when I'd been a boy, called in for a lecture.

"No," I said. "Because I can understand only too well what you did."

"I'm glad to hear that," he said. "I'm glad to know you have enough loyalty not to denounce me."

"Denounce you?" I repeated, and something went dead in me. "I hadn't even arrived at that point. I haven't figured out yet if it's my duty to keep silent or . . ."

"Then don't bother," he said. "I'd hate to have you lose sleep over it. Because I didn't kill Butworth."

"San!" I almost yelled at him, but the stranger's hand was pressing on my shoulder more forcefully now. "As long as you don't deny it. I just told you I could understand only too well. If I'd caught her . . . I'd have done the same thing. I know I would. I love you, San. Don't lie to me. You've got to take me into your confidence or our relationship . . ."

"Let's keep personal emotions out."

"I'm sorry," I said. "You're right. But you reacted emotionally. Well, never mind. You're lying to me, and that's what counts. Because you never did."

"I'm not lying."

"But you are. I saw Melinda and she told me."

"You saw Melinda?"

"On Saturday."

"You fool," he said. "You goddamn fool!"

"She told me all about it, about the man with the beard and the wig. You didn't recognize him, did you? You threatened to kill him."

He was very pale now. Not white, but a grayness that wiped away the rosiness of his cheeks, the deep red of his full lips. "That's true," he said. "And I meant it. I guess I didn't wring his neck then and there because I realized that I couldn't have my granddaughter witness the murder of a man. Her lover. By her grandfather. Enough had been destroyed."

"I admire your self-control," I said. "I don't think I'd have had it. I don't think I could have done what you did—go down to the kitchen, get a knife, leave by the back entrance and wait for him until he came down . . ."

"But I didn't," said San Angelo, and took a deep leisurely

swallow of the wine. "I went to my room and lay down on my bed, and cried. If you want to know the truth, that's it—I cried."

"So if you didn't kill Butworth, who did?"

"I don't know."

The stranger was moving away from me and across to San Angelo. He put a hand on his shoulder, just as he had laid a hand on mine. "The other day," San Angelo said, "we went through the people living in this house. Some of them have children. The crippled woman in the penthouse has three granddaughters, between ten and fourteen. And the biologist has a daughter. Eleven. Maybe Butworth . . ."

"I've no doubt Melinda wasn't the only one, but the fact is that on that night *you* saw him and Melinda together."

"Melinda had many friends. She might have talked. She's always liked to feel important, to be taken seriously, even to shock. She used to boast about you."

The stranger took his hand from San Angelo's shoulder and put it against his mouth. I recalled Ellen-Mary saying Melinda had told her I'd kissed her, "for real." "It's our fault," I said. "Yours and mine. She grew up without a mother, among men, except for some hateful governess who certainly never contributed any motherly warmth. The door to her room was always open. She heard a lot of what was going on. Your affair with Corinne. My girls. She didn't have a chance to develop normally. Maybe all she wanted, subconsciously, was to impress us."

The stranger smiled, an enigmatic smile.

"I'm glad to hear you defend Melinda. It's almost impossible for me to understand the thing. I'm of the Old World, a dago. I grew up to believe that a woman's virtue was the most important thing in the world, the one miraculous present she could give a man. Her honor. And then, to see . . ." Again his face went gray. "When I was young," he went on, "Italians used to live on what is now known as Hester Street. That's where I grew up. There wouldn't have been a man at the time, a father, a brother, any male relative, who wouldn't have . . . By the way, how is Melinda?"

"You should know," I said, "since you're the only one she's allowed to write to. You forbade her any contact with the outside world. She can't see anyone. Her mail is censored. Most of it never leaves that damned school you sent her to."

"And how did you manage to get in touch with her?"

"Never mind. What good do you think that sort of punishment is going to do her? It'll only make her more rebellious. She can't stay there, and I'm going to get her out, if it's the last thing I do. I have friends in Switzerland, good people. In Klosters. Fresh air and skiing, and a good Swiss school. If you're determined to keep her out of the States, they'll do a lot more for her than her present surroundings."

The stranger, still standing beside San Angelo, shook his head. I realized I'd got away from the point I was trying to make. San Angelo had turned slyly from the issue of murder to his granddaughter. "There was something about Clarissa," he was saying, "that I never liked. I know Justo loved her. So did you. But with all her beauty . . . she was like a perfect fruit, in which no one suspects a maggot, but it was there. Just as it is in her grandmother. A tiny spot, at the stem, which looks like a continuation of the stem, but isn't."

"Nothing is perfect," I said stupidly.

"I know. But everything doesn't have to contain the seeds of rot. One has illusions, and when one is old, they are perhaps all that is left. I wanted Melinda perfect, according to *my* conceptions of perfection. Goddammit, who could expect sex to be that strong in a little girl? Or maybe it wasn't. That bastard aroused it."

"And so, because he killed your dream, you killed him."

He shook his head. "Dear Tad, I learned long ago to keep my emotions under control."

"There are moments when we forget what we've learned. Believe me, I understand. I told you before that I did. He deserved it. But does Melinda deserve to be punished in a

way that won't help her but only make her more audacious?
You simply can't face the memory of her, naked, in bed
with a man."

"It's hard to face, granted," he said, "but I'd rather face
it for the rest of my life than endanger her. As you have
endangered her by going to see her."

"I don't know what you're driving at."

He said with great contempt. "You don't have as good a
brain as I've credited you with. Did it ever occur to you
that, for all we know, and we know only one thing with
certainty, that she"—he was having trouble putting it into
words—"that Butworth made her have sexual relations
with him. True, she didn't know who he was. For her he was
an elderly man with graying hair and a neat little Vandyke
beard. Thank God none of the pictures of him in disguise
got into the papers; thank the Lord it was in the interest
of Washington to keep them from the public. If she had
seen them . . . can you imagine . . . But I don't want to
dwell on that. What we have to keep in mind is that if
Butworth was after minors to satisfy his needs, someone else
must know about it. No man can keep such perverseness a
complete secret. If anyone should uncover his derangement
—and I say derangement on purpose—and find out that
Melinda was one of his victims, she would be put on the
stand by those people who have been waiting for a long
time to discredit the Administration. Butworth, a close
friend of the President, an adviser, a man he appointed to
the Supreme Court. I want Melinda far away from the
possibility of any such exposure. I want to keep her safe.
But you had to go and see her." His face had turned scarlet,
and he loosened his shirt collar.

"I still don't see why seeing her could possibly endanger
her."

"You've made yourself suspect," he said. "Instead of sticking to your assignment, you went off on your own. You saw
Jenkins and Momford."

"Within my normal functions."

The stranger smiled, and I kept quiet. "You went to see Walter Snipe; you took the trouble to meet Caroline Butworth."

"You know a lot."

"So do other people," said San Angelo. "The ones who want to protect the President from scandal and those who are eager for it. And when, after all that, you took a plane to Italy to see Melinda, and returned forty-eight hours later, what conclusions do you think will be drawn? By all means, let us get Melinda away from Rome. I wonder if Switzerland is safe enough. Chile or Brazil might be better. No President should be embarrassed just because he has put his trust in someone who didn't deserve it, and no little girl should be dragged through such slime. I'm sorry I ever loaned you to the commission."

Accused of stupidity, I was furious; I was also furious that San Angelo knew every step I'd taken. That he was aware of my relationship to Caroline. I had been in a strange mood of conflict before coming here tonight—elated that I had succeeded in what I had set out to do and deeply depressed at the same time over what I had found out. It was almost unbearable to see the man who had been my idol transformed into a murderer. His denying it instead of saying proudly, as I had expected him to do, "Yes. I did it and would do it again," robbed him of all the dignity with which I had always endowed him.

"I don't believe you," I said. "I still believe you killed Butworth."

"Poor Tad," he said, with a condescension that struck me as evil. "You came here convinced that you had found the murderer, and you still have nothing more than the motive."

The stranger laughed quite loudly then, a laugh that chilled my bones, and he was at the door when I hailed a cab, and got in with me.

CHAPTER

NINETEEN

HE WAS STILL THERE when I entered my apartment, very quiet while I poured myself a nightcap; and without saying a word, he followed me upstairs to the alcove above the studio. When I pulled the covers over me, he was still there. "Go away," I told him. "Leave me alone." I turned off the light, but he wouldn't move. Instead he sat down on my bed.

"What are you so upset about?" he asked. "That San Angelo didn't admit to the murder? How could he? How could he possibly confess to you? Maybe he confessed to the priest, that day in Connecticut, when you first learned that Melinda was going to be sent to Italy. What was his name again? Father Cenci. And he was so happy with the fat check San Angelo had given him for his parish."

I closed my eyes. I hadn't suspected San Angelo then. When had the first suspicion entered my mind? Had I become suspicious only after my visit to Walter Snipe?

I tossed restlessly. I felt empty, a spent shell. An emptiness that frightened me more than the three thugs in the parking lot had. I switched on the lamp again and lit a cigarette. I never smoked a pipe in bed. The stranger was still there, a blurred shadow. He was smiling, a wise yet smug smile, a smile you wanted to wipe off his face because its superiority was unbearable. "Never mind," he said soothingly, as if he were aware of my fear. "I know how you feel. Ever since you saw Snipe, you have been hounded by fear for San Angelo. You have seen him on trial, condemned for life. You have argued his case in court. Endlessly. How could you prove insanity? You had no motive, not until Ellen-Mary turned up at your apartment. You went to Italy to see Melinda and your relief when she mentioned the photos outweighed the horror of what she had to tell. Now you had something to show the jury—if and when to influence their opinion. You could hope for a verdict based on mitigating circumstances. It eased some of the shock. And tonight you went to see him, to tell him you had the proof that could justify what he had done. But he denied it. He didn't trust you.

"But let's look at it from another viewpoint. No, don't interrupt me. Isn't it worth something to you to be able to prove that the motive behind Butworth's murder was not political, was not born of the violence with which people react today to the restrictions of the law? Perhaps you have achieved something after all. The motive serves your purpose."

I lay there in a cold sweat. Yes, I could use the photos for my own purpose. It was an election year. The publication of the reason why Justice Butworth had been murdered would certainly strike the public—those for and those against him as proof that all crimes were not politically motivated. It might do a lot toward embarrassing an Administration that was trying to get restrictive laws enacted on the basis of political rebellion.

"But I can't use the photos," I screamed at the stranger. "Not for my own purpose. And expose the child. And think what it would do to San Angelo. And to Caroline."

I looked at the stranger. Suddenly his face was quite clear, like that of someone you know you have met in the past and can't place. I groped in my mind for the occasion when we had been introduced, shaken hands. I could feel the touch of his hand, a strong, warm hand on which all the fingers were the same size, like on an old painting, before the middle finger was given its proper length.

The stranger got up. He was my size. He had dark hair like mine. His eyes were the same dark blue. And he wore glasses. I hadn't noticed the glasses before. "But I know you," I said. And there was the annoying smile again, pulling at the corners of his mouth, the lower lip a little heavier than the upper.

"Indeed you do," he replied. "And the time has come for you to get better acquainted with yourself."

A fire truck went by, all sirens screaming.

CHAPTER

TWENTY

"**H**OW ARE YOU, DARLING?"
Caroline didn't like to be called darling. She said it reminded her of obscure dress shops that smelled of cheap perfume, and fat, middle-aged ladies telling her the gown, or whatever it was, did something for her. But I was too absorbed to think of another way to address her. Finally, this morning, the package from Italy had arrived, and at once I had called Caroline to ask if I could send over a messenger boy, and would she please hold the delivery for me until I arrived, later that afternoon. Then I scribbled on the strong manila envelope in large red letters: "Property of Thaddeus J. Wood. Do not open," slipped it into a large envelope and addressed it to her. Messenger boys are rarely held up, but I worried for hours about its safe arrival. Only because I had not wanted Caroline to become curious had I restrained myself from calling her again to make sure the package hadn't been lost.

"You look ghastly," she said. "You should have stayed abroad and taken a few days off. You need a holiday, Tad, from whatever you're doing. What's the matter with your lip?"

"I slipped and hit a stone."

"A stone?"

The noise the monkey and Tiger were making saved me from another lie. "They like each other," said Caroline. "When I take Tiger out, the monkey insists on coming with us. He rides on Tiger's back. And here in the studio, his favorite game is to catch Tiger by the tail and try to drag him around, and Tiger takes it like a lamb."

I spotted my envelope on the dining table. Nobody had tinkered with it, and I opened it, putting a match to the thin string of the first envelope instead of unknotting it or asking for scissors.

"I shot quite a few pictures of them," Caroline was saying. "With my Bell and Howell. A movie. Is there anything I can get you, Tad? Tea? Coffee? A drink?"

"Nothing, thanks. But I would like to use your lab, if you don't mind."

"Oh, you took some pictures too," she said, looking at the roll in its yellow carton. "Here, give it to me. I'll do it for you."

"I'd like to do it myself."

"Do you know how?"

"I was using my bathroom as a lab before you were born," I told her. "Just tell me the solution that's best for Kodak."

"Black and white or colored?"

"Black and white."

"Microdol X. There's a bottle of it on the shelf. To the left."

"Fix me a martini," I said. "Very dry and ice cold. You'd better put some ice in the glasses and put the glasses in the icebox for a while. You think you can do that?"

"I'll try. I didn't know you liked martinis. You never had one when I was around. Gin or vodka? Olive or lemon peel?"

"Vodka. And some of those tiny onions, if you have them."

"That's called a Gibson, isn't it?"

"All right. A vodka Gibson." And I'm afraid I slammed the door of the lab behind me. One could be too precise even when one was trying to please. Women, I thought, were always precise at the wrong time.

My hands were unsteady, and I almost forgot to switch off the bright light that would have ruined the exposed film. I turned it off, loaded the tank, and turned the light back on. I poured the Microdol X into the tank, tapped it to shake the bubbles from the film, and agitated the tank carefully every thirty seconds. I called out to Caroline, "How long do I leave them in the tank?"

"Not quite ten minutes, and then thirty seconds in the stop bath and about five or six minutes in the hypo."

The top of the hypo had been screwed on so tight, it took me a few minutes to get it loosened. I was hot and cold all over. And I itched. As if I'd eaten something I was allergic to. Chocolates. Chocolates always made me break out. I was longing for the martini, when Caroline's voice came again. "I think your time's up. You can take them out now, Tad, and rinse them. Rinse them for twenty minutes before you hang them up to dry." And then I took a look at them. The outline of a man and a woman. Melinda, a woman?

But she was. With small, beautifully rounded breasts, set high and a child's belly. If you wanted to be critical, perhaps the upper part of her body was a little too short. Two faces. Nose crushed against nose in a violent kiss. And another—Butworth again, well recognizable, standing up. And one under the shower. Drops of water gushing down on their interlocked bodies. I'd never taken a shower with a woman. Melinda, kneeling over a long, well-proportioned body.

I didn't want to see any more.

Caroline's voice again. "They'll need half an hour to dry. Why don't you . . ."

I interrupted her. "I'd like to make some prints."

"All right. I guess you should use high contrast paper.

Number four. Top drawer, left. And for a developer, Dectol. Above you on the shelf. Dilute the stock solution, two to one. Do you really want prints? Won't the negatives do?"

"No."

I began to get things ready. I found the paper. "I want the enlarger." She told me where it was. I smoked a cigarette. Two. My hands were still shaky. I was glad of the respite. My hands calmed down. I fed the negatives into the frame. I turned the machine, focused for a minute, but the picture turned black. Memory unexpectedly came back, from my school days, so I didn't have to ask her what to do next. I cut the exposer in half. This time I was lucky. There was a fair print. The rest were all right too. I put them on the easel. Finally, when they were dry, I used the hypo again for three minutes, rinsed them and shoved them into the blotter roll.

Caroline must have been listening to every move I made, and timing me. "You can turn on a safe light," she said, opening the door. She was holding a glass, filled with the martini I'd asked her to make. "If you'd rather have it in there?"

"No. I'll join you in a moment." I needed a few minutes to compose myself.

She was sitting on the waterbed, drinking her vodka straight. I could tell by the glass she was using. Mine was high-stemmed, two onions swimming on top like the eyes of a fish, a long time dead and faded by the sun.

"Okay?"

I took a sip—"Fine"—and tossed it down and asked if there was more. She rose, went over to the table and picked up a little bellied carafe with a sieve at the top. When she came back to pour me some more, I noticed that her usual quick strides were slower, sluggish, as if she were tired. "Don't you want anything?"

"I've already had three drinks."

"You usually have only two."

"Yes," she said. "Usually. But I felt like a third tonight, and I think I'll change my mind and have another after all."

Again she got up and walked through the studio in that strange, slow, almost cautious way, and when she came back to me she put the photo of Butworth, the one Melinda had given me, that showed him with the wig and the neat little Vandyke beard, between us on the waterbed. As she sat down, the mattress moved, and the glossy picture waved up and down, slightly distorting Butworth's features.

"Where did you get that?" she asked.

I had put the portrait upside down on the envelope. I'd meant to shove it back in, but I'd been in too great a hurry to get to the lab. It never occurred to me that she might pick it up. Never curious, often not even interested in what was mine . . . or me. I just stared at her.

"I opened the balcony door," she said. "It caused a draft, the photo fell from the table, right side up. Where did you get it?"

I decided to play it by ear, by instinct rather. Much the same thing, except that intonation and expression can betray you. "Why? Is it of any interest to you?"

"I asked you where you got it?" The urgency to know rose in her voice but subsided at once. Above playing any tricks, she added calmly, "I am aware of the fact that my father chose to disguise himself like that."

"I knew you knew."

"I didn't, until the police showed me the pictures that were taken in the park. I understand they were handed over to the FBI. But now there's one of him, here, enlarged too. Who gave it to you?"

"Melinda."

"Melinda?"

"You took her picture in that series you made of *People on Sunday*. With me behind her. You said I looked younger then, and you tore it up. Why?"

"I always destroy photos I don't need any longer, and just keep the negative on file."

"How well did you know Melinda?"

"I didn't know her at all."

"Do you happen to know if your father saw that picture?"

"I haven't the slightest idea. He may have." Her face was like a window over which a blind had been drawn. "What are you driving at?"

"After he was found murdered, you were interrogated. You told me so yourself. You were asked a lot of questions— as to his friends, his habits. Did you tell them about his deviations?"

"I regard privacy as one of the prerogatives of existence."

"But were you aware of his sexual deviations?"

"He is dead," she said, as she had said once before. "What does it matter?"

I tried to make a dent in her resignation, or if it wasn't resignation, in her determination to keep the thing to herself. "It matters to me."

"I'm sorry, but you don't matter, I mean, not in this respect."

"The FBI knows," I said, "and God knows how many other people. Or the investigation into your father's murder wouldn't have been called off. They told you to keep whatever you knew to yourself, didn't they?"

"They didn't have to tell me that."

"But they did. And you promised. Look here, Caroline, your father used your studio as a place to bring up girls, minors, children. And he photographed them right here, with your camera. You gave him the key to your apartment, you told me so yourself. Did you know what he was using it for?"

She didn't answer. Her face was still shaded.

"Didn't you guess?"

She looked at me then, and I wished the shade hadn't

been lifted. The anguish in her face was almost unbearable. "Tad," she said, "if I'd known, I'd have stopped him." And then, "Those pictures in there, that you wanted to develop yourself . . ."

"In the blotter roll. But I don't think you want to look at them."

To my surprise, she got up and went into the lab. She stayed there a long time. If I'm not mistaken, I heard her vomit, for she let the water run over the drainage for a few minutes. But when she reentered the studio, she came toward the waterbed with a strained, conventional smile, perfectly composed. She didn't sit down next to me, but drew up the uncomfortable little stool, as if she needed discomfort to remain upright. "I loved my father," she said, and then her hands fell open, palms up, in that ageless gesture of the poor and desperate. I longed to kiss those palms, to be of some physical comfort to her, to make her know how close we were, in spite of everything. But before I could she made them into fists, then opened them again, closed them.

"You loved him," I said. "But he also frightened you. Remember? You told me he frightened you. Why? How?"

"Why must I tell you?"

"I think it would help. Both of us. Did he try to make love to you?"

"No. Not actually."

"How old were you?"

She reacted to the direct question as I'd hoped she would. "Nine, going on ten. No. Ten, going on eleven."

"Where did it happen?"

"In his study."

"What were you doing in his study?"

"Saying good night."

"You always said good night to him?"

"Always. Even if he wasn't home when I went to bed, I'd lie awake and listen for the door. Maybe I fell asleep, but it must have been lightly, because I always heard him. And when I did, I'd rush downstairs."

She spoke like someone in a trance, or someone who had wanted to talk about some past event for a long time and been prevented by an innate loyalty and an old-fashioned shyness about sexual matters.

"So you went down to say good night to him, and what did he do?"

"On that particular night, he was having a nightcap and a ham sandwich. There was always a ham sandwich for him in the icebox, for when he came home late. He used to get it out himself and settle down in front of the fireplace with a bourbon and ginger ale. He liked a fire. I often lit it for him because I loved it too."

"Where was your mother?"

"Asleep. Maybe. Or out playing bridge."

"So you rushed down to kiss him good night?"

"Yes, I rushed down, and I remember I fell. I tripped over my nightgown and fell down the last two steps. He picked me up and asked me if I'd hurt myself. He carried me into the den and sat down in the armchair he liked best, by the fire, and sat me on his lap and caressed my knee. It was quite red. And then he touched my breast, no, not my breast, my nipple."

"And how did you respond?"

"I drew back. Instinctively. I had the feeling it was wrong. I said, don't Daddy. Then he wet his forefinger and drew a circle around my nipple, and said, 'It doesn't tickle anymore now, does it? That's what men will do to you when you're grown-up, so why shouldn't I?' And he pulled up the hem of my nightgown and looked at me. Mother had always told me never to let anybody see my private parts. And I was terribly ashamed."

"And then?"

"Then he put his hand down there. He wore a ring. Mother used to tell him not to wear it, that rings weren't becoming to a man who was a man. She said it rather nastily. But he liked that wide gold band with an amethyst set in it. The ring hurt me, and I screamed. I don't know if I screamed because of the pain, which wasn't really bad, or because his face looked so funny, so different. Quite unlike him. After that he held me close for a while, and I began to think it hadn't happened, everything was so normal again. Only he seemed terribly restless and depressed, and I asked him if he had troubles, and he said, plenty, and talked for a while and very interestingly, about his work, with all its responsibilities, almost as if they were too much for him. Then he seemed to realize suddenly how late it was and said, 'Off with you,' and as I got off his knee, he said, 'Darling, I love you very much, but you must never tell anyone about what happened between us tonight, not even your mummy. Promise?' I knew he wasn't referring to our talk, but to what had gone before. And I promised. And I kept my promise." And that, beloved, I thought, is why you are still a virgin. You are afraid of men.

"I'm glad you told me."

"But I shouldn't have."

She stopped. I told her to go on. She took a sip from her almost empty glass. Now her face was completely unguarded, her mouth was alive.

"He never tried to embarrass me again," she went on. "But then something happened. In Alabama. We had a quite large farm, with blacks in the fields, of course. There was a little girl. She used to come up to the house with her mother to clean. He always called her into his room to give her candy. And then, she slashed her wrists. She was about eleven. Her mother said that somebody'd been 'foolin' round with her.' That was the way she put it. The child had said, 'He too big. He hurt me.'"

She closed her eyes. In a while she opened them, and now they were clear, almost serene. "I began to read up on it."

"Read up on what?"

"Why older men molest little girls. It seems that some men can't derive satisfaction from grown women. They're afraid of them." She shrugged. "It's almost as simple as all that. And the only way they can find pleasure, is with a child, an innocent girl. Whom they can mold to their desires. Stress is often supposed to be at the bottom of it. It's a frailty. And you know, once I began to understand the thing, I could love him again."

We had reached such a point of intimacy, that I rose and sat down next to her. I took her face in both hands and held it, held it so close, I could see my face mirrored in her eyes. And just as I was about to kiss her, her lips parted, but not to offer them to me. Instead she said in a very energetic, sober voice, "Tad, let's destroy those photos in the lab."

I let her face slip from my hand and drew back. I shook my head.

"Why not?" she said. "You know about me, you know about Melinda, you know why my father was murdered. What earthly use are they to you now?"

I spoke too quickly when I said, "I might need them." I almost mentioned my conviction that San Angelo had killed her father, but I caught myself.

"You can't use those pictures," she said, with a calm as profound as the ocean. "I don't care what you need them for, you can't do it to me, nor to Melinda, and most certainly not to my father. I told you I loved my father. I am still his daughter and I still love him. Whatever weaknesses he may have had, you can't use them for any purposes of your own." And with that she got up and made a dash for the lab.

I was quicker than she, but I doubt if I could have prevented her from getting into the lab first if the doorbell hadn't rung just then. It stopped her for a moment, and I got there ahead of her and stuffed the photos and negatives in my pocket.

It was Per, the man to whom she was so grateful for having given her a chance to illustrate his travelogues.

Caroline, her face still white, introduced him as Mr. Gunnarsen. We shook hands, and I asked him if he was the famous Gunnarsen whose satirical drawings had been amusing the world for years. No, he said, and that he'd only come up for a nightcap, and to ask Caroline if she'd go to Hong Kong with him.

"Anywhere you like," said Caroline. "I'll make you a cup of coffee."

He accepted her offer, and I sat down with him at the dining table and told him I couldn't understand why he'd chosen to go to Greece with the Junta in power, torturing people who had the courage to protest a military dictatorship.

"We got some pictures," he said, "of boys who had been tied down and beaten on the soles of their feet until they were clumps of raw meat that sprang the leather of their shoes. Caroline has a way with authorities. I'd never have come up with half as realistic a job without her. They let her visit prisons. She shoots out of her pocket. I don't think you've read my book. I was quite vehement about a lot of things nobody wanted to hear. I'm not exactly *persona grata* right now in the United States because I've attacked the Administration for its delivery of arms and financing of mercenaries, but can you tell me, Mr. Wood, where I could work today without running into things we abhor? I've made a study of some of your prisons. Do you really think mixing arsenic in the food of black prisoners, not enough to kill them, mind you, just enough to keep them vomiting day and night, is more recommendable? Oh yes, you have penal institutions that are show places. I forget how many. I'm never any good at figures unless I check back. Which I do when my galleys come in. And Japan? India? England? Well, England may still rank as one of the best. But France? Where is a man to go? You have to accept a certain degree of depravity, but it's the degree that matters."

He took a couple of dice out of his large pocket and began

to roll them around and around. "You can attack Sweden, if
you like. We have the same problems. Ten-year-old whores
soliciting on street corners. Narcotics. Alcohol. You name it.
A progressive prison system, yes. Some prisoners even have
private cells and a key. They can go to work, study at
schools close to their houses of detention. Repeats? Many.
God, I don't know what I'm talking about, all I know is that
one's got to go on living and working, regardless of what
happens. I fought in World War Two. You know what it
taught me? Survive! Whatever happens, survive. And that
you can't change human nature. I lost a lot of money running a farm. I bought the place for some children I'd
adopted, twelve, all from different nations. It didn't work.
And I tried my damnedest. One murderer, three thieves,
four whores, two runaways. I can't even recall what happened to the rest. You have to bend with the wind. I won't
give you an argument, so don't start one. I have to work in
order to live, and I like to live. And that's all I have to say
for myself. Now that girl in the kitchen, she isn't real. She's
an illusion. That's why I like to have her around. Just so's I
know that across the mountain there's something with no
pollution of the soul."

"I was brought up to look upon Swedes as rather dour,
not willing to express themselves."

"Sorry if I bored you."

"Not at all. Please go on. I enjoy listening to you." But he
took the large cup of coffee Caroline served him and seemed
to have said his say. "A small one for you?" she asked. "Or
would you rather go to sleep without thinking?"

"I've done all my thinking."

She didn't respond. She turned to Gunnarsen. "When do
we leave?"

"In two weeks. If you can make it. I signed the contract
today."

"Congratulations." She held out her hand. "Two weeks.

You couldn't give me three? I have a lot of work to finish off."

"Okay," he said. "In that case I'll fly out and you join me later. I'll get a place ready for you. Did you ever run into the Thompsons? He used to work in the Congo. He's set up his own business. Diamonds. Shall I buy you a beautiful necklace?"

I let them talk without interfering with their feeble jokes or asking who the people were they mentioned. I was busy with my own thoughts and was determined to outstay Per Gunnarsen. I certainly didn't want to leave them together, to give him a chance to take Caroline in his arms. Tonight, if I could trust my instinct, she wouldn't resist him.

We had a couple of Aquavits with the coffee she kept bringing out of the kitchen, and some cookies Gunnarsen found in one of the tins on the shelf. Left-over Christmas cookies, plain molasses decorated with almonds or dried plums. And then, all at once, she ushered us out. With the gentlest but most determined smile. "Boys, I'm ready to drop. Per, call me in the morning. But not before nine. I need some sleep. Tad, are you going to take Tiger home with you, then I don't have to walk him?"

"Of course. Thanks for taking care of him. What about the monkey?"

"Let me have the monkey until I leave. I've grown very fond of him."

Walking down the stairs, I asked Gunnarsen where he lived. "One Fifth Avenue," he said. "Too expensive for me, but the rooms are large, and I don't bump into a wall with every move I make."

I had my car outside, but I didn't offer him a lift. There was a group of boys milling around at the corner. I didn't like their looks, so when Gunnarsen hailed a taxi, I asked him, "Would you mind dropping me?" I'd feel a lot safer with him along. The garage could pick up my car in the morning.

I walked Tiger around the block before I went in. Opposite my house there again were some boys, sitting on the front steps of a small brownstone. "Watch it Tiger," I told the dog, before I put my key in the lock. He reared up and roared. Once inside, I made straight for my revolver. It was still in my desk. Loaded, as I'd left it. I took it upstairs. Again I couldn't sleep. All the noises to which I had grown accustomed in the three years I had lived here seemed strange and suspicious. The dripping of the faucet in the kitchen, the creaking of the stairs as their wood settled back, the sound of the handles of the door to the patio withstanding the pressure of the wind, the slightest sound from anywhere, and I would sit up and reach for my gun. Finally I gave up all efforts to rest. Usually I left my apartment at eight forty, to be at the office at nine, but now, when morning came, I got up and dressed and was on the street by seven.

I walked up Greenwich Avenue and found a coffeeshop, just opening. The coffee tasted like dishwater and the eggs weren't done the way I liked, but the toast was all right and I ate it with plenty of jelly and a Danish that had just been delivered. I sat for a while on Washington Square, on a bench that was still partly whole, and wished I was a child again, enjoying a game of marbles. But only dirty words were scrawled in front of me on the soft ground, above them a dove, with "Peace" scribbled on its spread wings. Time passed slowly. I was the first person to enter the bank at nine, a branch of the Chase Manhattan where they didn't know me. I rented a safe deposit box and heaved a sigh of relief when I finally had negatives and prints under lock and key. I called Caroline from a booth five blocks up. "Did you destroy them?" she asked, without a good morning or anything.

"No."

"Then don't call me again until you have." There was

silence on both ends of the line, then we hung up. Simultaneously.

Father Cenci lived in his parish east of Broadway, not far from Foley Square. On my way to him I made sure again that I wasn't being followed. He was sweeping around the altar of his little church. The boy who was supposed to come and clean hadn't turned up.

"There were only a few people for mass this morning," he said, not in the least surprised to see me. For a moment I wasn't even sure he'd recognized me, but then he leaned his worn old broom against a pillar and came to sit beside me on the pew I'd chosen.

I pulled out a small envelope, with the key, and when I pulled it out, I realized that he could see the mouth of my gun, which I'd taken along. He didn't remark on it. "I want you to do me a favor," I told him. "Keep this for me, and take good care of it. You may open it only if San Angelo is arrested. It may save his life."

"San Angelo arrested?"

Somebody besides me had to know. Not Jenkins, not Momford, and certainly not Caroline. Somebody who was not involved. So I told him everything. He listened with his hands folded across his narrow chest, so quietly, that I thought I was sitting next to a man who had died in his sleep. And when I was through, he didn't shake his head or make any gesture that might have betrayed his thoughts. "Didn't San Angelo confess to you, weeks . . . almost two months ago?"

"Confessions," he said, "are between a man and his God."

"He denies having anything to do with the murder."

"And why don't you take his word?"

"Everything points to him."

He said nothing.

"Will you take these keys, please, and follow my instructions? I told the bank about you; they have your name."

He held out his hand and the envelope with the keys disappeared in the folds of his soutane.

"If anything should happen to me, Father, I want to ask you one more favor. There's a girl, Caroline Butworth, the Justice's daughter. Go and see her. Tell her what I've just told you."

"I will," he said, and made the sign of the cross over me.

CHAPTER

TWENTY-ONE

WHENEVER I CALLED CAROLINE, our exchange of words was the same. She asked me if I had destroyed the photos; I replied that I had not, then she hung up. But each time her voice was a little more eager, carrying the hope that surely I had finally done what she wanted, and I guess mine was too, with the anticipation that she might have come to accept my attitude. And our silences were a little longer with disappointment.

Of San Angelo I saw hardly anything. At first I thought he was too busy to find time for me, then I began to realize that he was avoiding me on purpose. No invitations for lunch, no questions as to whether I intended to join him in the country, no evening chess games, and when we met by chance on our way from one room to another, he would pass me hastily, with barely a greeting. I couldn't tell if my accusation had hurt him deeply or if he was putting on some sort of act that happened to suit his purpose. He could play almost any part, and I had often been amused over how he could fake fury or calm or wide-eyed innocence when he thought a situation called for any such reactions. But if he was hurt, so was I. Not only had he misunderstood me completely, he was now withholding his confidence from me.

Then, one day, I found a memo on my desk. He would appreciate it if I would put in an appearance at a party one of our clients was giving. Gerald Mamert. Ten o'clock. Black tie.

San Angelo loved parties. The atmosphere of festivity, the chance to meet people. It always surprised me that a man his age would trouble, after a long day's hard work, to take a bath, shave again, change, and become part of a noisy crowd. Now I tried to tell myself that I should devote the evening to the shabby little office another lawyer, John Hunter, and I had rented on Eighth Street and Second Avenue, three steep flights up, where people who couldn't afford legal advice could bring their problems without having to pay a fee, but when I thought of the old lady who had been evicted after thirty years of living in the same house, and the unresponsiveness of her landlord, case pending, of the young conscientious objector who was being harassed by his draftboard, of the old man who had been picked up as a pusher, although he swore he had never carried as much as an aspirin on him—it all seemed too depressing. And Mamert, after all, was a client. In oil. Nor did I want to be rude to San Angelo. On the contrary—the party might give me an opportunity to ease the estrangement between us.

Mamert's apartment was one of those typical old-fashioned barracks on Upper Park Avenue. Huge, and without individuality. Most of the furniture was arranged to accommodate as many guests as possible. But the ceilings were high, giving an illusion of freedom, and the spread in the dining room was formidable. About a hundred people were milling around, some of them dancing in the big square entrance hall, where the carpet had been taken up. A band was playing rock 'n' roll. An extra man, with a guitar, was wandering around, strumming close to whatever group he had selected as a random audience. Butlers were serving drinks and white-aproned maids kept offering appetizingly arranged trays with hot and cold hors d'oeuvres. One attracted my attention, little squares of toast with red and black caviar. They formed a mosaic, and I hesitated to disturb the pattern, when a hand reached past me and did. I knew that hand, its long, delicate back, the elongated fingers, the way it moved so quickly and determinedly. Caroline.

There is an expression—"My heart leaped in my throat." I had never experienced it, now I knew it was more than a cliché. She looked quite different. But then, I had never seen her in anything but jeans, with bare feet and a shirt or sweater. Her feet were still as good as bare. She was wearing low-heeled sandals, laced up to her knees. You could see her legs, well-shaped, exciting, through the long see-through skirt she was wearing over very short, tight-fitting pants. About three inches of flesh showed between her belt and the hem of the top. And she was made up. A few weeks ago, when I had first met her, I had wondered what her eyes would look like if she put some mascara on her long, colorless lashes. Now I could see. And the effect was resplendent. It wasn't overdone, either. Just the faintest shade of green on the eyelids, the fragile pink of rose on her cheeks, a less pale shade of rouge on her wide, generous mouth. She had tucked an orchid in her hair. Somehow it made her look frivolous. Before I could say anything, a voice to my left greeted me. "Hi," said Per, very handsome in a dark blue dinner jacket which suited him even better than the corduroy jumpsuit in which I had seen him last. "Isn't she gorgeous? I finally got her to let a Japanese friend of mine make up her face." He put a possessive arm around her waist and away they danced.

I remained standing where I was, feeling left out, angry, and jealous. Somebody said, "Don't they look well together? I understand he doesn't have much money." Somebody else said, "She really shouldn't go to parties so soon after her father's death." And whispers about Butworth.

Caroline danced with abandon. I hadn't known she liked

to dance, or even danced at all. She had seemed too severe, too rigidly set in her disciplines to enjoy the normal pleasures of her age. Watching her move through a routine that seemed to me a self-invented dance, I was convinced suddenly that she had lied to me when she had said she had never been close to a man. Her body seemed perfectly attuned to Per's, and although there was never a vulgar motion between them, an aura of sensuality issued from them. I tried to talk to a lady who gave the impression of a statue hung with jewelry to compensate for whatever the artist hadn't been able to supply. I made some polite remarks to my hostess, a thin nervous woman with a laugh pitched too high and too full of trite talk to distract me. I had a second drink, and a third, and I watched San Angelo watching Caroline. Did he know her? Had they met? He wouldn't volunteer any information unless I asked him directly. I couldn't bring myself to do so.

Dinner was announced, and people began to stream into the dining room, and returned with plates overloaded, as if from a smörgasbord in a Swedish restaurant. I got myself some smoked trout and looked down the line to see if I could spot Caroline and offer to get some food for her. But she was still dancing. Tables had appeared in every room, covered with blue felt, with blue candles and pink carnations. Although I am not naturally rude, I decided not to sit down anywhere, and the moment I saw Caroline leave Per, I handed my plate to a passing maid and walked up to her. "May I get you something to eat?"

"Per is looking after me."

"Then may I have this dance?"

There were still quite a few people trying to get to the buffet, and some still dancing, most of them within earshot. It would have been too much of an affront to turn me down. But she tried, politely. "I'm really quite tired. I haven't danced in such a long time." I simply put my arms around her and led her back into the middle of the dance floor.

"Would you like something less tiring? A tango or a waltz? I could ask the band . . ."

"I never learned to waltz or tango."

I laid my hand on the bare spot of her skin. To my delight I could feel it shiver. "Don't hold me quite so close."

I left more space between us but kept my hand where it was. "Caroline."

"I'm leaving in ten days," she said, said it in a way that conveyed this was all the time I had to change my mind. "I had my first injection two days ago. No bad reaction, either."

"And when are you coming back?"

"No idea."

"Then you want me to pick up the monkey."

"I'll have him dropped at your apartment. I'll call Rose to make sure there's somebody there."

"Don't you think," I said, "that you owe me an hour or so, to talk to you?"

"I don't owe you anything."

"I didn't mean it that way. I simply want to talk to you when neither of us is feeling emotional."

"Tad, I'll always be emotional about my father. I can't help it. Rationalizing won't change it. Even if I could understand you, I wouldn't allow it to sway me. I'd feel like a traitor all my life."

"So would I."

"For God's sake, Tad, why?"

"I can't tell you. I'm sorry."

"So am I."

After a while I said, "Will you call me to say good-bye? I do want your address, to be able to reach you."

"If you want me to."

She waved to Per, who was leaning against a wall, two heaped platters in his hands. I let her escape and spent the rest of the evening talking to my host about his oil leases, and to another guy who was in difficulty with railroads. I danced with two quite pretty young girls, one an archaeologist who was going back to Turkey in the spring; the other was doing volunteer work with retarded children. There was a doctor, who had set up hospitals for the insane in South America and other parts of the world, and spoke interestingly about such secret societies as the Poru, Zoe, and Bundu, and the influence they asserted in Liberia. I even took a hand at one of the three bridge tables that had been set up in a den and to which, much to the annoyance of the hostess, several men had retired.

When I looked for Caroline, I couldn't find her anywhere and assumed she had left. A little while later I saw San Angelo get up to go and hurried after him. I was only too glad to leave and to have an opportunity, perhaps, to speak to him about the night I had accused him. On the street, when the doorman asked if he should whistle a taxi for us, San said, no, he'd rather walk. He didn't ask me to accompany him, but I didn't want him to walk home by himself on the almost deserted streets, six blocks down to Seventy-seventh. A sharp wind was blowing and he coughed. I didn't like the cough, and the fact that it worried me made me realize all over again how devoted I was to him. Somehow our relationship had to be restored, however disastrous the events that lay behind us.

"Nice evening," he said finally, in an obvious effort to make conversation. "Good cigars, good wine, and delightful champagne. Never had anything as good as that mushroom salad. Must tell Mrs. Riley about it. And Mamert is a fool. I wouldn't risk that kind of money in Kuwait, not right now." And then, "Your friend is very attractive."

"What friend?"

"The Butworth girl. Charming. Full of spirit. Going off though, isn't she? I had quite a talk with her. Even a dance."

I had missed seeing them together, talking as well as dancing. Somehow it chilled me. Caroline dancing with the murderer of her father, unaware that our break centered around him.

By the time we stopped in front of his house, it was three o'clock in the morning, and not a taxi in sight. I didn't want to leave him, not yet. I had taken Tiger out before leaving for the party and I kept a suit and overnight things in my old room for occasions like this. "If you don't mind, I'd like to stay the night."

He nodded. But if I had been hoping for a chance to talk to him at length, I didn't get it. He went straight to his bedroom, and I to mine, after I had fixed myself a nightcap to take upstairs. I switched on the radio. It was the same one that Justo had given me on my fourteenth birthday, but it still worked. The tune to which I had danced with Caroline came over the air and I lay there, arms behind my head, listening to the music and thinking of how beautiful she had looked and the way she had danced with Gunnarsen. And now she was going off with him, to a strange exciting city. I had never been in Hong Kong, only read about it or listened to people who had been stationed there or gone there on business. I tried to imagine what it would be like to travel with Caroline in parts of the world both of us didn't know. I must have fallen asleep, dozed off rather, while still composing a letter to her in my mind, for suddenly I sat up, alert and frightened. There was a sound I couldn't quite make out, but it was definitely a sound I wasn't used to. It came from the window. A few seconds later I knew what it was. Somebody was throwing something, sand or little stones, against the pane. I turned off the light, got out of bed, and moved cautiously to the window. I parted the curtain.

My window looked out onto a small courtyard which had a door to the street, locked these days, and chained for greater security. Each tenant had a key to it in case of emergency. There was also a fire escape, just as in Caroline's studio, rusty iron steps, which you could reach from my room. For years now there had been a debate as to whether Holmes protection shouldn't be installed on this particular window. The agency had recommended it. "Just a few strips of paper." But since it would have prevented the opening of

the window except for a few inches, and the small room
could get very stuffy, it had never been done. San Angelo
wasn't afraid of burglars. In his opinion, anyone who really
wanted to get in would find a way, and he always kept three
hundred dollars in cash to give to anyone who might force
entry. He was convinced he could talk them out of bashing
him over the head as long as he offered them the cash with a
promise not to give a description to the police, and that it
was much more important to be able to get out of the house
and into the courtyard in case of fire.

I couldn't see anybody. I knew, from having lived in that
room so many years, that there was another fire escape running down the building next door, also ending in a small
courtyard which was separated from us by a tall iron gate.
There was a light over the back entrance of the basement,
and gradually, as my eyes got used to the semidarkness, I
realized that the shape cowering below me was a man, hud-
dled over so that he looked lifeless. A sack.

"Who are you?" I asked. "What do you want?"

I don't think I really expected an answer to my stupid
questions, but the sack straightened up. "It's me," a voice
said, but because the words were whispered, I couldn't tell
to whom the voice belonged. And then, still in a whisper but
this time clearly audible, "Doug."

"Doug?" For a moment I had difficulty remembering who
Doug was.

"Doug Farmer from next door."

"Hi," I said. "What on earth are you doing there, Doug?
Did you throw some stones against my window?"

"Just some sand from a pile down here."

I couldn't see any pile, but I knew that some repair work
was being done next door. The workmen must have left it,
possibly to mix cement.

"Why throw sand and wake me up? Do you want something?"

He was shaking his head violently, almost spastically.
"No, no. I thought Melinda was back."

"Melinda? But this isn't her room."

"I know. But she used it sometimes."

"Did she? Well, she isn't back. And I don't know when she will be. You'd better go home. It's ice cold. D'you want to catch pneumonia?"

"I'm warm," he said. "Hot as they come." He straightened up, took one fumbling step. "Watch it," I called out. "You'll break your neck."

"Oh, no, I won't," he said, and for a second I saw his face, white, round. "I'm a bird. I can fly," and he took off into the darkness below. Gone. "Doug!"

I heard the heavy thud with which he landed. "Are you all right?"

"Perfect," he said. "I'm one person you don't have to worry about."

I closed the window, drew the shade, then the curtains. I turned off the radio, which was still playing. But I didn't go back to bed. I sat down at the desk of my childhood days and began a letter to Caroline, a letter I had to write, to get some of the things I felt out of me, but which I knew I would never mail.

CHAPTER

TWENTY-TWO

I T HAPPENED ON FIFTH AVENUE. A week later. And in broad
daylight. To be exact, at one twenty on a Thursday. It
was one of those days with an illusion of spring in the
air. You had to tell yourself it was still January or you might
have expected buds to burst and leaves to take shape
miraculously on the bare, black branches. The sun was shin-
ing and the temperature was in the high forties. A late
January thaw.

I'd gone to Fifty-eighth Street East to pick up one of our
foremost sociologists and take him to lunch. His "Compara-
tive Study of the Influence of Terror on the Judiciary" was
overdue. I wasn't exactly in a good mood, but I wasn't depressed either. Melinda had left Rome for Switzerland and
was staying with my friends in Klosters, experiencing the
Alps for the first time and the wide-open runs of the Par-
senn. Her letters weren't censored anymore, and she had
sent me an enthusiastic cable. "Thank you, darling Tad. This
is where it's at. Why don't you come? I'll give you my bed
and make do with my sleeping bag. The Thompsons say
you're welcome any time." It ran over the twenty-five words
allowed for a night letter, but I could see her shrug as she
counted them. So what. So what, indeed!

With Caroline, no change. Whenever I'd call up, she'd ask, "Destroyed?" I'd answer, "No," and she'd hang up.

A man came up to me, a laborer. Hard hat, jeans, a heavy sweater. Too warm for this mild day. An unlit cigarette hung between his lips. "Got a match, Mister?"

I fumbled in my pocket and got out my lighter, worked it for him and held it to his cigarette. "Thanks," he said, stuck one hand in his pocket and let me see the revolver. "Just walk quietly. Cross with the light and stop when I tell you or you'll be a corpse."

There were hundreds of people milling around—secretaries, clerks, and their bosses, returning to their offices or leaving for lunch. A construction going up on my left, with men on bulldozers, manipulating them as if they were bucking bronchos. A police car, parked, one guy apparently asleep, the other talking on the phone. And children. About a dozen in double file. A school outing. Probably on their way to Central Park.

"Get going," the man said. His mouth was a narrow line. He'd dropped the cigarette.

I glanced over my shoulder and in a showcase saw the reflection of another guy in a hard hat, sweater, and jeans. I took three steps, tentatively. To my left was the oyster bar of the Plaza, where they knew me. If I could duck into it . . . But before I could make it, there was another man, hard hat, sweater, jeans, blocking me, silently but effectively. Still I tried. I said to the doorman, "Tell Mr. San Angelo . . ."

"Keep going," said the man who has stopped me for a light. "Just keep going, Mister, and a bit faster if you don't mind."

I couldn't believe it. I knew people were being abducted, but surely not at one or two P.M. on Fifth Avenue. It usually happened at night. They'd jump you from out of dark doorways or stop their cars and yank you in. I put one leg before the other, a mechanical doll. From Schwarz, no doubt. Trying to cross the avenue with the light. Maybe I should have crossed against the light, or thrown myself in front of one of the cars turning slowly into a cross-town street. "Keep moving."

The showcases of Bergdorf Goodman displaying antiques. Elegant clothes for women. Somebody shoved me, gently but surely, into a green station wagon parked at the curb—I hadn't noticed it—under a sign that said NO PARKING. Shoved me into the back, between the first man who had stopped me and the one who had prevented me from entering the restaurant. The man at the wheel wore a beret. He was chewing on an unlit cigar. The place next to him was empty. Somebody shoved me down on the floor of the car, put something into my mouth. A gag. My arms were being pinned back by handcuffs. The car took off. I thought— Rose will take care of Tiger, and the monkey is still with Caroline. If she calls, Rose will tell her that I haven't been home since . . . maybe it will delay Caroline's departure. Maybe she'll stay long enough to find out . . . A blindfold was fastened over my eyes, the gag was pushed deeper into my mouth, then I couldn't think anymore. Somebody hit me and I blacked out.

I woke. And for a few blessed minutes had no recollection of what had happened. Memory returned gradually. The restaurant, where I had lunched with the famous sociologist whose paper was overdue. He had promised me faithfully I'd have it by the end of next week. The day had been springlike. I had walked down Fifty-third Street on my way to Saks to buy a few shirts. No. That had been another day. My jaw felt sore, my eyes hurt. There was something heavy on them. Heavy as a hard hat. And then I knew. I shook my head to help clear it, and something fell away. Something cold and damp. When I could open my eyes, I saw what it was. Ice bags. And there was a bucket filled with ice next to me on a small table, and a carafe with water. Also my favorite brand of tobacco, which I always bought at Dunhill's. And, thank God, a bottle of bourbon. Full. My brand.

It didn't make sense. Nothing made sense. But the fact

that my abductors knew what I liked to drink and smoke startled me. The room I had been put in was narrow but quite long, shaped like a towel. It must have been a passage once, a wide one, a hall, perhaps, now with walls at either end. The one facing me had a door in it. There were two windows, set too high to look out. Both barred with iron grillwork. One comfortable, worn armchair, a writing desk with a chair in front of it, an old oak cupboard, rather high. It reminded me of a cupboard we'd had in my father's house, and of the day when Cook, angry with me for some reason or other, had put me on top of it. I had never felt as helpless in my life as in that half hour before Mother heard me, wailing above her, and had taken me down and fired the cook.

The bed on which I lay seemed all right. I prodded the mattress. Not too soft. Only then did I discover that my hands were no longer tied, and my legs free to move. It came as a surprise. I looked at my right wrist to find out what time it was. My watch had stopped at one thirty. I reached for the bourbon with the feeling that it mightn't be the best thing to have alcohol right then, but I didn't care. I found my pipe, unbroken, in my pocket and filled it from the fresh tin. My teeth didn't seem to work right. They wouldn't close correctly over the stem of the pipe nor would my mouth close over the rim of the glass the way it should have. Some of the liquor ran out of the corners of my mouth. A drooling baby.

Had there been a fight? Had I offered resistance at some time or other? I couldn't remember. All I knew was that the left hook in the car couldn't have caused all this damage. The room, which seemed to have everything, did not have a mirror.

I put down the glass and the pipe onto the ashtray so considerately furnished by my hosts. I got up. I walked across the room. I tried the door. It was locked. I moved the armchair in front of one of the windows, but even standing on it, the window was still too high for me to see anything

but the bare crowns of trees. I hadn't the slightest idea
where I was. I had blacked out the moment the man had hit
me.

I forced myself to do fifty knee bends, keeping my head as
immobile as possible. Then I shadowboxed for a while.
When my body had limbered up, I went back to bed. I
refilled the ice bags and put one on my jaw, the other over
my right eye. I noticed only then that my glasses hadn't been
broken. They were lying, intact, on the table next to the
bourbon and tobacco. So was my briefcase. There was no
bathroom, but a pan under my bed. I used it. Then I must
have fallen asleep, because when I woke again it was dark
in the room, and I couldn't remember if there had been a
lamp on the desk or a ceiling light. I got up again and felt
along the walls and after a while found a switch, and a light
in the ceiling went on, shaded by a multicolored Tiffany
glass shade, the kind that were all the rage now. The light
did something for me. It brought two events into clear focus
—the robbery in Caroline's studio and the attack on me at
Kennedy. Undoubtedly they were connected. But I had no
time to dwell on the conclusion because there was a noise at
the door, then it opened. The man with the beret who had
driven the car stood on the threshold, gun in hand.

"Come in," I said. "Don't just stand there. Tell me what
you want."

He didn't answer, but he moved an inch or so to let a
woman enter, a woman carrying a tray.

"I brought you some food," she said. "Try to eat, even if it
hurts."

"Why Mrs. Johnson," I said, "what are you doing here?"
And for a moment I thought that, like me, she had been
abducted.

"Well, somebody had to cook for you."

She put the tray down on the desk and smiled. All I could
do was stare at her dumbly. Ridiculous as it was, I was filled
with anger at the thought that I had lost the most efficient
secretary I had ever had. I had planned to persuade her to

take a job with the firm once our work for the commission was finished, Q-tips, nasal drip, and all. And how could I ever finish that little assignment without her? Then the full impact of her presence here hit me. "What *does* all this mean?" I asked her.

"Patience," she said. "You'll soon find out."

The "you" did it. She'd given herself away. "Try to eat," she said again. "I'm afraid it's rather mushy, but tomorrow you'll be able to eat solids. And your jaw isn't broken, in case you're worried. So you don't have to be afraid to use it even if it's sore."

"Great God! You're in on all this."

She smiled again, cheerfully. "Just knock when you're ready for coffee."

She was at the door when I caught her by the elbow. "Listen here—you can't walk out without an explanation."

"I told you to have patience, Mr. Wood." She shook herself free. "In due course you'll know. Now don't be childish." She moved away and out through the door, and the man with the beret closed and locked it. I could hear the key turn twice and a chain being anchored.

I forced myself to eat. I swallowed some very good home-made pea soup, a soft broiled hamburger, mashed potatoes, jello, telling myself with every bite that all I could do was have patience, that it was utterly useless to speculate as to who the people were who were holding me prisoner. But what did they want from me? Could they possibly know about the photos?

When I was ready, I did as I'd been told—I knocked on the door. This time Mrs. Johnson didn't appear, just the man. He shoved the tray with the coffee through the open door and closed it immediately.

I shouldn't have had the coffee. It kept me awake. I took "The Minority Data of the Systemic Conditions of Political Aggression" out of my suitcase, and although some of it was interesting and would probably be useful, I couldn't seem to take in what I was reading. I had a couple of bourbons and was feeling pleasantly groggy when the door opened again. "If you want to wash up . . ."

My guard, in spite of his heavy build, had a quite finely cut, intelligent face and an educated, well-modulated voice. I wondered what he did when he wasn't abducting people and guarding them. He made me walk in front of him, hands over my head, out of the room and into a bathroom. It had a tub, the kind you find in old farmhouses, on legs, with a gas stove above. But it was big enough to stretch out in and the stove worked. Just as in a hotel, there was every-thing—a new piece of soap, still in its wrapper, a toothbrush in a plastic case, toothpaste, Kleenex, no electric outlet but utensils for shaving, and towels hanging over thick pipes which warmed them, as in English hotels. I took advantage of it all. I lingered over my bath, I brushed my teeth as thoroughly as if I were going to the dentist, I shaved, I found a nail file in the small medicine chest above the washbowl and filed my nails, and all the time panic gnawed at my insides like a rat cornered somewhere in my body. By now Rose should have gone home at whatever time she chose, without wondering when I'd be in. I hoped to God she'd let Tiger out. Caroline wouldn't call, and San Angelo hardly ever phoned my apartment after office hours. He was not the one to intrude on one's private time. And tomorrow morning there wouldn't be anyone trying to contact me ei-ther. Rose would come in, let Tiger out . . . and the day after? More or less the same thing. The day after that, though, was pay day, and Rose might call Caroline and tell her that I hadn't been home for two nights, and where was I? But I doubted if Caroline would be sufficiently concerned to call Foley Square, where nobody would answer, or San Angelo's office. On the third day, San Angelo might ask his secretary to phone, in the meantime Tiger's barking and whining had probably disturbed the neighbors, but nobody would know that I'd been picked up by three strangers and driven—where?

I was led out of the bathroom and back to my room the same way, hands over my head, a gun at my back, in complete silence. The trays had been removed, the ashtrays emptied, the ice container refilled, a table lamp put on my bedside table and the ceiling light switched off. As far as service was concerned, you couldn't ask for anything better.

I think it was because of the difference in lighting that I didn't notice him at once. I saw him only when he spoke. He was sitting at the far end of the room, in the comfortable armchair. A young man, about my height, light hair, crew cut. The FBI man whose help I had requested. "Momford!"

"You sound surprised."

"I am."

As he moved to change his position slightly, I noticed the bulge under his jacket. Even though I had to recognize the fact, I couldn't help doubting it. "So *you* had me abducted?"

"I left the service," he said, instead of answering my question, "and am working for a private group now."

"When?"

"About ten days ago."

"And it's in the interest of this private group that you're here?"

"Yes."

"What do they want?"

"If you're too tired to discuss it now, we can postpone it until tomorrow."

"No. Thanks to you I've had a good rest. More than I usually get on a working day."

"Let's cut the irony," he said. It wasn't an order. It sounded more like friendly advice.

"Okay with me. Then perhaps you'll answer the question I asked you. Why?"

"Butworth. You happen to know something we would like to know."

"I'm sure you know as much as I do, if not more."

"I expressed myself badly. We think you are in possession of something we need."

"Who is we?"

"For the moment let's just say—important people."

"Drink?" I asked, pouring myself three inches of bourbon on some rocks.

He declined. Just his eyebrows went up, creating two triangles on his forehead. He didn't look any longer like a man who would choose real estate as a career. "And they may be able to save your life."

"My life? What are you talking about?"

"You must be aware," he said, emphasizing every word, "that at any moment now you may be arrested as Butworth's murderer."

"Butworth's murderer? You're out of your mind! I didn't kill Butworth."

"That's what every murderer says."

"Well, I didn't. What's more, I have a perfect alibi for the night he was killed. A witness, too. My girlfriend. I was with her that night."

"Your former girlfriend, you mean." He said it with his eyes on me. "What if Susy chooses not to remember?"

I took a big swallow and swirled it around inside my mouth for a moment or two. He had Susy all wrong. She wasn't vindictive. Nor dishonest. But it made me uncomfortable to realize he knew about my affair with Susanne, and that I'd called her Susy, and that we'd broken off.

"Our conclusion is that it was you."

"And how did you arrive at this conclusion?"

"You were enraged when you found out."

"Found out what?"

"Look," he said. "Let's put our cards on the table. I at least am willing to do so. Perhaps it will be easier for you to play along with us if I tell you what we know. First: we have come across some unsavory facts in Butworth's past which have been hushed up for years. He seems to have had difficulties with women and therefore fooled around with minors. Young girls. Children. Lately . . . that is to say during the last few years, he seems to have restrained himself. At least we couldn't find anything. Until he met Melinda San Angelo. And when you discovered that Melinda and he . . ."

"Melinda?" What did he know about Melinda? Had he seen her? Talked to her? I poured myself another drink. It tasted sour, and I had some trouble swallowing it.

"Your godchild," he said, and now his mouth was wide, all teeth showing, even and white. "It is understandable that you were enraged. You went to the San Angelo apartment that night . . ."

"I did not. I never left my apartment on Tenth Street that night."

He shrugged. "Your behavior since then. Your obsessive interest in Butworth's murder. Your visit to Jenkins to find out what they had unearthed. You saw Snipe."

He paused significantly, and all at once I knew that the strange little man who had given me such valuable information had been killed by Momford, or on his orders. But I didn't say anything. Momford's next words deepened my conviction, "And when he told you that the investigation had not been stopped but was being pursued by a third party, and that the killer lived in San Angelo's apartment house, you left New York and flew to Rome."

"I saw a client."

"You also saw Melinda."

He knew. It wasn't put as a question.

"If you are so sure that I am the murderer, then why all this nonsense of trailing me, of having me brought here, and keeping me under guard? Why not have me arrested, which would be so much simpler?"

"That isn't what we're interested in. We couldn't care less whether you killed Butworth or not. We want the proof you have of his sexual deviations."

"I have no proof."

"Melinda gave you something."

"She gave me nothing."

"Oh yes, she did. She gave you a small package."

"Oh. You mean the present for her grandfather."

"She gave you some photos."

"Nonsense! She did nothing of the sort."

He shifted his position. "Come off it, Wood. By now you must realize that we've been watching every move you make. Yes, we slipped up once. We were not able to relieve you of that package in Rome, and at Kennedy, unfortunately, you no longer had it on you."

He paused, watching my face closely. I was unhappily aware of the fact that I was no longer in control of my breathing, which was anything but even.

"Meanwhile," he went on, "we showed one of the photos in our files, with Butworth wearing the wig and beard he used on—shall we say his little escapades?—to Ellen-Mary Mellon. In my experience all children can be made to talk. She recognized him instantly, although she tried to deny it. But her face gave her away. All we could get out of her though was: Ask Mr. Wood. He knows. So here we are, Mr. Wood, with the more or less logical conclusion that you have proof . . . photos, letters, that might save you from a long prison sentence, or even your life. If you made a deal . . ."

I played it dumb. "Made a deal?"

"Yes. A deal. You know as well as I do that Washington is interested in keeping the motive behind Butworth's murder a secret. Should you come under suspicion, you could threaten Washington with the material. On the other hand, there are certain men who would be only too happy to prosecute and embarrass the Administration."

"Your people."

"Yes."

I filled my pipe. Insane. The whole thing. Completely insane. Yet how close it came to the truth. All Momford had wrong was the murderer. If San Angelo had been arrested, I would have tried just what he had described.

"If that is your assumption," I said, striking a match, "how can you expect me to hand over to you the so-called proof that might give me a chance to stop a trial, or certainly get me off more easily?"

Momford got out of his chair. "Look," he said, "I, or rather, the group I'm working for want only one thing—to embarrass the Administration sufficiently to bring about a change. From top to bottom. In any case, with the Administration or with us—you're safe. It simply depends on whom you decide to sell out to. And my people are determined it shall be to them."

"Who are your people?"

"I'm not free to reveal their names, but you'll meet them, once you've handed us what we want. But I can assure you of one thing—they are just as powerful as anyone else you may have in mind. All you have to do is come to a decision, the right decision as far as we are concerned."

The irony of it all made me laugh. Because I had made my decision long ago.

"And if I don't?"

"There are ways to make a man tell."

The idea of torture was not appealing. I had often wondered how a man could stand up under it. Everything I had read—about eyelids torn from your eyes, electrodes stuck in your ears, on your genitals, nails plucked from your fingers and toes, being tied in a helpless bundle and hung upside down until the rush of blood to your head drove you crazy. It was all right there, opposite me, in the person of Momford, a threat I had to face as real.

"I'll have to think it over."

"Do," he said pleasantly. "But I advise you not to be a fool. You won't get out of here until we have what we want." And with that he left me. Again the key turning, the clanging of a chain, familiar sounds by now.

I lay down on the bed. Now it mattered little that the

mattress was to my liking. So this too, I thought, was a way
of making politics, only that it hardly ever got into the history books. I tried to think what would happen if, indeed, I
was charged with murder, and for a while tried to figure out
whom I would choose to defend me. There were quite a few
men who'd never lost a case. And Susanne—would she let
me down? If they paid enough? How far could I rely on
her? The Rileys would be no good as witnesses. Butworth
had been killed on their night out. They couldn't testify if I
had come to the house or not. I had a key and could come
and go as I pleased. Then the idea struck me that all the
thinking I was doing was futile. I would never get out of
here. Momford's pleasant tone, so dispassionate, no anger,
not even irritation, his conviction that I had what they
wanted . . . it all led down another track. How could I have
been so stupid as to think that I was the only one who had
found out? They had gone to the same sources. Jenkins,
Caroline, Snipe, Ellen-Mary, the convent, with one advantage I hadn't had—their knowledge of Butworth's sexual
deviation. A feeling of guilt overwhelmed me. If I hadn't
rushed off to see Melinda, if I had succeeded in persuading
San Angelo to let her come back to the States, biding my
time to question her . . . and I could hear San Angelo's
furious voice, calling me a goddamn fool for going to Rome.
He had been right. As usual. I had led Momford to Melinda.

And finally, the thought of death.

Death always came to other people, never to you. That
was what made people go on, the confidence that what happened to others couldn't happen to them, at least not for a
long time. And there was little time left. Was I ready to die?
Was anyone ever ready to die? Even decrepit old people
fought to stay alive. And what would my death achieve?
Momford's "group" wouldn't get the material they were
after, but was I willing to die for that?

The night was long, dark, and silent. I fell asleep, woke,
fell asleep again, plagued by nightmares, exhausted by help-

lessness, guilt and fear. I must have just dozed off when I opened my eyes again to a sound I hadn't heard before. A wind had sprung up. It was whipping some of the branches of a tree outside against my window. I lay there listening, and the sound changed, became irregular, became the sound of small stones or sand being thrown against my window. The window of my room in San Angelo's apartment. And I could see Doug's face on the fire escape, a white round face, like a little moon that had fallen suddenly onto the steep, rusty steps, and I could hear his voice, his loud voice answering my question, "Do you want something?" with "I thought Melinda was back." And myself, saying something about this not being her room, and clear as a bell, his answer, "I know. But she used it sometimes."

How had he known that Melinda used my room?

Had Melinda boasted to Doug that she had somebody better? A real man? Or had Ellen-Mary told him about Freddy?

I couldn't lie still any longer. I got up and paced the room. And there was Melinda, sitting on the cold stone bench in the convent garden, shaking her head in answer to my question—had she ever told anyone about Freddy? Doug, for instance? I had been too upset to watch her face when she had denied it. What if I was wrong, and San Angelo had never run out after the man he had discovered in bed with Melinda but instead had really gone to his room, to weep. "And why don't you take his word?" Father Cenci had asked.

And the branches kept whipping against the window, and Doug's voice rose to a scream that filled the room. "But she used it sometimes."

CHAPTER

TWENTY-THREE

AT EIGHT O'CLOCK NEXT MORNING, the man with the beret unlocked the door. He remained standing on the threshold, holding a tray with one hand, the other in his pocket, on a gun, no doubt. I took the tray from him and put it on the desk. I used the trick they had used to stop me on Fifth Avenue. While pouring coffee into the cup, I asked him if he had a match. "My lighter doesn't work."

"They never do."

He took a step toward me and I swung around and threw the boiling coffee in his face. The one moment of pain and consternation sufficed for me to attack him. Though his hand with the weapon shot up, he was blinded momentarily and I could twist his arm back, at the same time I brought my left knee up against his groin. The gun fell on the carpeted floor, but I didn't dare to reach for it before I had knocked him out. During the night I'd torn one of the bed sheets into strips, and I bound and gagged him, and for good measure hit him once more, hard, against the jaw.

With his gun in my right hand, I felt less helpless and made my way cautiously out of the door and into the passage. To my left was the bathroom, to my right a corridor that led into a kitchen. Dirty breakfast dishes were standing

on a linoleum-covered table. Two cups, two plates. Somebody else had to be around. I spotted him through the window above the sink. He was scattering sand from a bag onto
the icy path outside. I stepped away from the window and
opened the kitchen door a crack. I crouched next to it, on
the floor. I whistled softly and a moment later heard his
heavy steps approaching. The second he entered, I grabbed
his legs. In his effort to reach for his revolver and keep his
balance, he fell backward, his head hitting the tiled floor
with a thud. Before I used a potholder to gag him and the
kitchen towels to tie his hands and feet, I took off his red
and black checked lumber jacket. He never made a move.
Now if there weren't any others, I had to cope only with
Mrs. Johnson and Momford. But since I couldn't hear a
sound anywhere, I wasted no time looking for them. I went
outside. Under an overhang I saw several pairs of skis, leaning against the wall of the house. I chose the longest ones,
undoubtedly Momford's. It was difficult to fasten the bind-
ing over my ordinary shoes but finally the spring closed, and
reaching for a pair of sticks, I propelled myself forward and
along the narrow cleared path that ran downhill. It would
have been impossible to make any headway without the
skis, but at any moment now Momford, getting up and looking out of a window, might see me. I was glad I had thought
of taking the jacket off the man. It would confuse Momford.
At least restrain him from shooting until he had made sure.
On the other hand, he might by now have gone down to my
room, found me gone and be after me. Below me was a
stand of trees, and as soon as I had reached it, I dared to
turn around and glance up at the house. No sign of activity,
just smoke curling blue in the cold air. The hill I had just
come down was empty.

I dared to get back on the cleared path. A little while
later it ran through dense woods and steeply downhill. Once
a deer crossed ahead of me into the darker safety of the
trees. At one point I discovered the tracks of a sled which

must have got stuck in a snowbank. Footprints were clearly visible in the snow. Had I been brought to the house on a sled? And had it been here that I had decided to fight? After about two miles, my left ski came off, and I couldn't refasten it. But I had skied on one before. Then, suddenly, it was flat country and directly in front of me stood a small farm. A boy came out of one of the barns and I stopped him and asked where the next bus stop was. "Three miles down the road."

I had been left my wallet, and pulled it out. "Is there a car you could use? Could you drive me to the stop? I'll make it worth your while."

He hesitated. "Where you from?"

"I'm lost," I told him.

He looked down at my one ski, at my shoes, and shook his head. I held out a ten dollar bill. It made up his mind for him. He motioned me to follow him. I got into a small truck beside him. "Wish I had a snowmobile, like them." He pointed up the hill. All I could see was a yellow spot, headed in our direction. Until that moment I had congratulated myself on having made my getaway. Now fear came back. Momford won't shoot to kill, I told myself. I'm no good to them dead. At least that was what I wanted to believe. I threw the boy another bill as I pushed him out of the car. "You can pick up the truck at the stop." I stepped on the gas, skidded, straightened out, got out of the yard and onto the macadam road and drove like a madman, praying that the motor wouldn't stall, the tires hold up, that the snowmobile wouldn't overtake me.

On the outskirts of a town—Monroe, New York—I nearly ran down an old woman emptying her mailbox. A few minutes later I reached the highway and saw a parking lot, almost a semicircle, around a low restaurant. I drove the truck in, got out and made for the men's room. I took off the lumber jacket, rolled it up and left it in one of the booths. Not quite three minutes later, from the window of the washroom, I saw Momford leave his snowmobile on the other side of the highway and try to cross the cleared black asphalt to the restaurant. Traffic was heavy and he had to wait, which gave me a few extra moments. I pushed the window open, crawled through it, and was at the rear of the building while he was still weaving his way, through angrily tooting cars, to the front.

There was a black Pontiac. A woman was just getting in. I leaped across the few yards separating me from her, tore open the door, and got in beside her before she could drive off. She looked scared to death and ready to scream. I put one hand gently over her mouth. "This isn't a hold-up," I told her. "Don't be afraid. Just drive out of here as fast as you can."

She was so terrified, she obeyed. Someone must have told her that the best thing to do in a situation like this was to offer no resistance. I kept my hand over her lips until we were a few miles from the restaurant. Then I showed her my identification card and explained that I was on a government assignment. "The Butworth case."

"What Butworth?"

The simple question made me laugh hysterically. "A Justice of the Supreme Court who was murdered about seven weeks ago."

It was the wrong thing to say. She changed color and gripped the steering wheel so hard, her knuckles showed white. Apparently she believed she had a killer in her car, in spite of which she drove well and as fast as the speed limit permitted. Then, just as I was beginning to relax, she veered sharply to the right and stopped the car in front of a state police station. A patrol car was standing in front of it and a state trooper got out when she honked loudly and incessantly.

"What's the trouble, lady?"

She pointed at me, sputtering out her story, and the trooper told me I'd better follow him. He was just as little impressed by the name Butworth as she had been, and it seemed the height of absurdity that what had been the content of my life for so many weeks should never even have been heard of here, fifty-eight miles from New York. A sign we had passed had given that distance. But my personal card impressed them. Police never like to make a false move with a lawyer. "Call my firm," I told one of the men, who was fumbling with my card. "The number's right here. Area code two one two. Murray Hill . . ." He looked offended, as if I were implying he was illiterate, and disappeared. I couldn't tell whether he'd called New York or not, nor did I ask him. It was enough for me that he asked me where I wanted to go, and when I told him, New York, he offered to drive me to the next bus stop. An hour and twenty minutes later I alighted at the Port Authority Bus Terminal.

CHAPTER

TWENTY-FOUR

I HAILED A TAXI and told the driver to drop me at Seventy-seventh and Madison. I walked into Schrafft's, crowded as always at this time of day, with old ladies, and young women with babies or dogs, nodded to the waitress, who knew me, got a cup of coffee, and was in the house next door to San Angelo's within a few minutes. The Farmers lived on the tenth floor. A maid let me in but looked doubtful when I asked if I could see Mrs. Farmer. "She never sees anybody on days like this." I didn't know what she meant.

"Tell her I'm here on account of her son."

She left me standing in the entrance hall, disappeared, and came back to usher me into a bright, chintzy living room. "Have a seat, please." I didn't sit down, but used the telephone, one of those new-fangled models which had the dial built into the receiver. Yellow like the walls, it looked like an incongruous flower in my hand. I called our free legal office and asked to talk to John Hunter. "John," I told him, "I need a bodyguard. The toughest guy you can find. Have him meet me at San Angelo's apartment as soon as he can make it."

"Dick Corbett," he said. "He's guarded . . ." and he reeled off some well-known names. "Anybody, just as long as he's efficient," I told him, then paced the room, looking at my watch, counting the minutes Mrs. Farmer needed to get ready to receive me.

I had never met Doug's mother before. In all the years Doug had been invited to Ridgefield for weekends, or to the house in New York, she had never taken the trouble to as much as write a note of thanks, or telephone, or make any effort to meet San Angelo, Melinda, or me. Melinda, though, had been at Doug's, and come back to say, "There's nothing in the ice box but flowers. His mother belongs to some garden club or other, and that's all she's interested in. That's why they can't keep help, and I think Doug would starve if he couldn't come here for dinner sometimes." So I had formed some kind of prejudice against her and was surprised now to see how pretty she was—pretty, faded, and frail. She aroused your protective instincts.

I had at least expected her to know, by name, who I was, but obviously she had no idea. Though I didn't want to waste any time on social amenities, I heard myself say, "I'm sorry to have to disturb you," but she seemed just as eager to come to the point and, motioning me to sit down, asked, "do you know where Doug is?"

Her question startled me. "Isn't he here? I mean, I know he must be in school right now, and I wanted to ask you—is he still going to the same school? I must talk to him. I'm Tad Wood. Melinda San Angelo's godfather. Doug's spent quite a lot of time with us, off and on."

It didn't register. She folded her hands as if in prayer. "He isn't in school," she said. "He hasn't been to school for days. I don't know how many. They called this morning, threatening not to take him back. He only has a year and a half more to go before college, and if they expel him . . . there isn't a school that would take him. You know, I guess that he's been expelled once already. From boarding school. I don't care if he goes to college or not, I really don't think we could drag him through four years of that, but I would like him to finish high school . . ."

It sounded strange like a repetition of what she had probably said endless times, to herself, to others, to Doug.

"Yes, naturally. I understand."

"But he's disappeared again."

"Disappeared?"

"Yes. It's almost a year now since he began making a habit of it. At first just a night, then two or three in a row, suddenly a whole week. Or more. I wonder if you know what a mother goes through, lying awake, imagining the worst. The things that can happen nowadays. He's my only son, my only child. He's taken up with such a strange crowd, or maybe they're all strange today. And nothing we've tried seems to work."

"What have you tried?"

"Well . . ." She was obviously at a loss. "We've sent him to the best schools. And camps." And with a sudden change of mood, "You didn't come here to tell me he was dead?"

A note of hysteria was clearly discernible in her voice. I reached out to pat her on the shoulder, to calm her, and she grasped my hand and clung to it with the strength of desperation.

"Nothing of the sort, Mrs. Farmer."

"Then why did you come?"

"I told you—it's essential for me to have a talk with Doug."

"He won't talk to you. He won't talk to anyone. And these last weeks he's been worse than ever. Listless, inattentive, impossibly depressive and depressing. My husband can't take it anymore. He clears out when Doug's here."

I finally said, matter-of-factly, "He's on drugs, of course. Do you know which one?"

For a moment she didn't answer, just looked at me, horrified. Then she said, "All I know is it's not heroin. I've looked when he was asleep and never found any needle marks."

"Did you ever think of sending him to a psychiatrist?"

"He went once, then he wouldn't go back. Oh Lord, if only I knew where he was."

"You said he's made a habit of disappearing."

"The last time it was two weeks. One day less than two weeks."

"Have you thought of police? They might find him."

"No, no." She shook her head vehemently. "We can't do that to him. He'd never forgive us. And then it would be in the papers. The publicity would break his father."

"Other boys get into trouble and their fathers stand up for them."

"Are you blaming us?" Anger colored her cheeks.

On the defensive suddenly, I didn't know what to say. Nothing came to my mind but trite phrases. "I'll try to find him for you."

Her mood changed again—"Would you? Do you think you can? I'd be so immensely grateful"—and changed once more. "But not if you have to bring in police. We can't afford a scandal. We just can't."

"But if it's for Doug's good?"

"No, no. Never. And I won't hear of having him institutionalized, either. That's come up several times."

She put both hands to her ears in a childish gesture, to blot out anything else I might have to say, then, quite unexpectedly, she left the room. I waited for a while, thinking she'd gone to collect herself and would return any minute, but after ten minutes she still hadn't come back. I took a photo of Doug, that was standing on the grand piano among other pictures, out of its silver frame, and left.

CHAPTER

TWENTY-FIVE

I LET MYSELF IN SAN ANGELO'S APARTMENT and went to the kitchen to tell the Rileys I was there and expecting a man by the name of Dick Corbett. They were having lunch and offered to make me a sandwich or scrambled eggs, anything I wanted, but all I wanted was some cheese and more coffee to keep me going. Then I called the superintendent and asked if I could speak to Ellen-Mary.

"Certainly, Mr. Wood. Any time. But she's in school right now. Won't be home until four, this being Friday. Why? Is anything wrong?"

I assured Mellon that I only wanted to give Ellen-Mary a message from Melinda, but asked where her school was located anyhow. Then I went into Melinda's room. There were all the prizes she had won in tennis tournaments and riding contests. Silver cups, all sizes, engraved with the dates of the event and kept dutifully shined by Mrs. Riley. A cord was strung above the headboard of her bed, with pictures attached to it, cut-outs from magazines, mostly rock artists, and one of the Beatles when they were still young and together. And stuffed animals—a bear, two dogs, a goose—all in atrocious colors, with horrible faces, which she had won at country fairs, or San Angelo and I had won for her. On top of the bookshelf lay the large photo album I had given her for her twelfth birthday. Dark green leather. And next to it, her diary, with a little key in it. I didn't open the diary but leafed through the album and took out every picture of Douglas Farmer. I called John again. "I need a detective. No, a private one. I'll send a messenger boy down to you with photos of the person I want traced." Photos. They had never meant anything to me, but at this point they seemed to be ruling my life.

When I came down in the hall, Dick Corbett was there. He looked his profession to such an extent, I was taken slightly aback. "Just call me Dick, Mister," he said. I told him to phone for a messenger and handed him the photos to give to him, I had put them into an envelope of Melinda's stationery, with a note to John, explaining what he should tell the detective. "And right now, Dick, I need an hour of sleep. Don't let anybody in, and if Mr. San Angelo should turn up before I'm awake, tell him you're a pal of mine. That goes for the Rileys too. And wake me at twenty to four."

He gave me a mock military salute and I went to my room, the room Melinda had "used sometimes," and fell on my bed. I was asleep before I could pull the covers over me.

Shortly after four, though, I was at the corner of Lexington Avenue, a block from Ellen-Mary's school. It was strange to have a guard. I had never been in need of protection, and the knowledge that someone was watching my every move made me self-conscious. Dick Corbett had a way of not being there when I looked for him, yet seemed always to be in front or behind me or at my side, as if he had split up into so and so many parts.

Ellen-Mary came out of school with a bunch of girls which broke up as soon as some boys became visible, then crowded together again to form an even bigger group. She saw me, took a few steps in my direction, then hesitated and waited for her pals to join her. I finally called her name and she left her group and trotted up to me. "I couldn't help it," she said belligerently.

"Couldn't help what?"

"Don't you know about the man who showed me Freddy's picture and asked thousands of questions? And it happened right here. He waylaid me on my way home from school."

"I think you behaved very well, Ellen-Mary."

"I didn't tell him anything. Just that you knew."

"That was the right thing to say."

"I didn't like the man."

"Oh, he's perfectly all right."

"Is he really? Snoopy, though. What do you want of me now?"

"I told your father . . ."

"You talked to my dad? And you promised . . ."

"Hold it," I said. "I only told him I wanted to see you because I had a message for you from Melinda."

"Nothing more?"

"I thought you trusted me."

"After that man showed me Freddy's picture, I changed my mind. How did he know where I lived? And what my name was?"

"I couldn't tell you."

"So what's Lindy's message?"

"Ellen-Mary, that was a ruse. I didn't want your father to know we were friends."

"What is it you want to know?"

Though her brashness was unpleasant, I couldn't help but admire her instinct. "Where do you get your pot, Ellen-Mary? Do you buy it?"

"Are you nuts, Mr. Wood? Where would I get the money? It's a present. Mostly, that is."

"From whom?"

"Friends."

"Like Doug?"

"I wouldn't take the garbage he likes."

"Why not?"

"Because it's dangerous. All chemicals are dangerous. I try to stay away from the hard stuff."

"Very sensible. And where does he get it?"

She shrugged.

"Around here or in the village?"

"You can get all the stuff you want all over town."

"But the village is where most kids go, isn't it?"

"I wouldn't know."

"But you do," I said, and then I lied. "Melinda said you knew, that sometimes you went with Doug . . ."

"She's making it up. She makes up a lot of things."

"She said Doug had a source in the village. He's disappeared again, you know."

"He doesn't disappear. He just prefers to hole in somewhere when he's on a bad trip."

"Where does he hole in?"

"Ask Melinda. She seems to know it all."

"Okay. I shall. She's coming home in a few days."

"Is she?" She sounded alarmed.

"I thought you'd be glad to know. You seemed so concerned about her."

Ellen-Mary shrugged. "Are you afraid she'll take Doug away from you?"

Her face clouded over, her mouth became small. You could see what a mean little woman she was going to be some day. "You're afraid he'll walk out on you when she gets back, aren't you?"

"He won't. I'll see to that. Why should Melinda have everything? Freddy. Doug. You."

She tried to run away, but I grabbed her arm. "You'd better tell me where Doug is or . . ."

"Or?" she repeated, challenging me.

"Or I'll tell your father everything you told me that night at my place."

"And I'll tell him you gave me some grass and smoked it with me."

"All right," I said. "We'll go straight to your parents . . ."

"You're hurting me, Mr. Wood."

I took my hand off her arm but grasped her hand firmly. "Come on, Ellen-Mary. Let's tell them everything. It's the only right thing to do."

She didn't open her mouth until we were standing in front of the house. Then, angry tears in her eyes, she said, "Jenny's. It's the place where kids hang out when they want to be undisturbed. That's all I know." I let go of her hand and she turned to face me. "Pig!" she said. "That's what you are—a pig!" And she ran into the house, slamming the door after her.

CHAPTER

TWENTY-SIX

W E WERE SITTING IN MY APARTMENT, Dick Corbett and
I, waiting for Detective Howard to call as soon as he
had located Jenny's place. Corbett was sitting at my
desk, playing solitaire. He had brought his own deck of
cards. "You can't read all the time," he said, shoving a
paperback into his wide coat pocket. "Mind if I use your
desk?" He didn't drink anything but beer. Three empty
cans stood in front of him, three more in the ice bucket on
the floor. "First thing I do in the morning is have a nice cold
glass of beer."

By now I knew his life story. He had been in the Marines,
then drifted across the country, trying his hand at odd jobs
here and there, and finally became a guard, first for a bank,
then for a department store. Only during the last three years
had he gone into private service. He was unmarried. "Can't
keep a wife straight with that kind of life. Too rarely at
home and then mostly too sleepy. Couldn't really blame a
woman for looking for company somewhere else, but why go
on a merry-go-round when there are enough girls you don't
have to pay alimony?"

He had prepared dinner from what Rose had left and
eaten an enormous steak while I told him what he had to

know and gave Tiger three-quarters of my meat because my jaw was still sore, and anyway, I wasn't hungry. I didn't feel like calling Caroline. I wanted to keep my mind on Doug. No distractions. But then she called me.

"Tad." And when she heard my voice, I could hear her sigh. "Thank God! I tried to reach you all last night, and this morning. Even at your office. Nobody knew where you were."

For a moment I could feel fear edging in. Had Momford, having lost me, tried to blackmail Caroline into revealing anything about the photos he could assume she knew about? "Are you in trouble?"

"No. Just very tired. I'm leaving tomorrow and there are a thousand things to do."

"Tomorrow?" And although, in a way, I was disappointed, I was glad she was getting out of the country, away from Momford and the Butworth case, if it should break.

"I can't give you my address yet," she was saying. "Per didn't fly ahead as planned. I guess American Express will have to do until I've found a place."

"You want me to pick up the monkey?"

"I've already deposited him with Rose. It was love at first sight."

So Snipe had been wrong about the monkey's aversion to black. Wrong, too, about the number of the house, if Doug . . . but tragically close enough.

"What time is your plane leaving?"

"Late afternoon. Around six." And after a slight pause, "I'm going to miss you."

"Do that," I said, happily surprised. "But I'll call you again. Good night. Sleep well."

I didn't want to keep my line busy in case Detective Howard called, but curiosity was too strong. I dialed Susanne's number. She answered on the first ring and I could tell by her voice that she'd been expecting somebody else. "Long time no hear."

"That's right. But I understand you've been questioned about me."

"Correct," she said. "For hours. Anybody would have fallen in love with you after what I told them."

"Could you be serious for a moment? Did they try to bribe you?"

A moment's hesitation, then she admitted, "Yes. And I said I'd give it some thought if they'd give me two million, cash, tax exempt. D'you mind terribly if I end this now? I'm expecting a call."

"I'd like to see you though."

"Any time. Any time. It was fun talking to you."

She left me with the pleasant impression that she'd found another man. Fast work. Or maybe she'd had somebody on ice and that was why she'd let it come to a showdown with me. Next I decided to let San Angelo know I was back in town. He seemed a little annoyed to be disturbed. Obviously he hadn't missed me. How could he have? Barely thirty-four hours had passed since I had last spoken to him. Yet it made me feel ridiculous. In that short space of time I'd gone through hell and come to a conclusion that might influence all our lives—his, Melinda's, Caroline's, and mine. And Doug's. Yet he wasn't aware of anything.

"Nothing wrong I hope?"

"Nothing," I said. "I just wanted to know how you are."

"Couldn't be better. I understand you were in this afternoon."

"I forgot a book last time I slept over."

"Coming out to the farm this weekend?"

"I might. I'll let you know."

After that there was nothing to do but wait. I had never been good at waiting. "Take a tranquilizer," Dick Corbett advised, as he watched me pacing restlessly. He pointed to his solitaire, four rows of thirteen cards each, spread out one below the other. "The Napoleon," he explained. "They say the guy used to play it in the evening, before a battle. In a tent. By candlelight. There's nothing like solitaire for clearing your mind and whiling the time away. At least I've never been able to find anything better. Try it some time." He opened another can of beer, his powerful fingers tearing the strip away from the can in one sure motion.

"I wonder why Howard hasn't called?"

"He will. He's a good man. Worked with him on several occasions. He always tracks down what the customer wants. Just give him time."

I should, I thought, have forced Ellen-Mary to reveal more than just a name. There were thousands of places where kids holed in when they wanted to be, as she had said, "undisturbed." In Harlem, on Riverside Drive, on West Seventy-first Street, on the Bowery, in Queens, in the Bronx, in the suburbs. Every address I had ever read in newspapers came to my mind, and there might be more than one with the same name. Jenny. Jenny's. Maybe the Phoenix House would know. But I had to trust Howard. He had sources I didn't. And for all I knew, Doug might be back home by now. I looked up the Farmer's number. Mrs. Farmer answered, and I could see her, sitting by the phone, hoping for some word of her son and at the same time afraid the news might be bad. I didn't mention my name but pretended to be one of her son's pals. "Doug there?"

"No, he isn't. Who is this? Do you want to leave a message?"

"No. It's okay." I hung up.

Did I have any idea what a mother went through, lying awake, plagued by fears about her only son? Even a mother who hadn't exactly been with it, like Mrs. Farmer? Perhaps riddled now, not only with apprehension but also with guilt? I didn't. But I knew what the Farmers would have to go through if I was right and their son had killed Justice Butworth. And suddenly panic closed in on me. What would be gained if I was able to establish Doug as the murderer? Melinda and Caroline would still be involved. Called in as witnesses. But then my mind cleared. Doug was sixteen. He would be tried in Youth Court. Press and public barred. His name would be mentioned, of course, and the fact that he had killed Butworth, but otherwise? The publicity could certainly be handled in a way that would not involve Melinda or Caroline.

I played a hand or two of gin with my bodyguard, hardly able to manage the small cards, but I had no others. Not at home. I played gin only with Melinda, in Connecticut, on rainy days when there was nothing else to do.

It was almost midnight before Howard called. "Got it," he said, and gave us an address in the village, east, and told us where to meet him.

He was a short man, older than I had anticipated. His bushy red hair showed some gray and his doll-like face was made smaller by wide sideburns. Dressed as he was, in blue jeans and something like a poncho instead of a jacket, he looked more like a hippie than the detective I had been expecting. "Piece of luck," he said. "Ran into a pal of mine. He gave me the code or I'd never have got in without calling the police."

We walked quickly up half a badly lit block and stopped at a building which looked uninhabited. It was a loft, with no light whatsoever coming from anywhere. The tinplate with a number on it was illegible, half the color had flaked off, so were those on the buildings next to it.

"I've been here already," Howard said, "and told Jenny I'd be back with some friends." He pressed a bell I couldn't see, nor did I know how many short or long rings he gave. Anyway, the door opened. From inside, darkness yawned at us. Howard shone a flashlight on stairs, some of them broken. "Five flights up."

Dick Corbett had a flashlight too, a more powerful one. "Excuse me," he said, as I put one foot on the first step. "Wouldn't surprise me to meet some of Momford's friends here." So he went first, then I, Howard following us. By this time I had forgotten all about Momford and his "private group." But of course Dick was right. They might try to get me any time, any place.

Five flights up stood a man, a type you see nowadays only in a circus. Under his striped sweater, his muscles were bulging. He was smoking two cigarettes at the same time, one in each corner of a repulsive, heavy mouth. Howard whispered something to him; he nodded and let us in through a door so flush with the wall, I hadn't noticed it. The room we entered was square and quite large. A candle flamed under a madonna in a niche, and several religious figures stood on tables, shelves, and chests. A stack of Bibles, books on Zen and assorted esoteric religions were piled on the floor. A radio was playing. From under a rosy light in one corner, a woman rose languidly. She had snow-white hair and ruddy cheeks and kind, round brown eyes. A mother figure if ever I saw one, but her leathery skin and the reddish-blue of her nose betrayed the alcoholic. She moved with difficulty, using a stick. It was over an inch wide, the kind that can hold a glass tube filled with liquor, an umbrella or, fastened to the handle inside, a knife. You couldn't believe in her game leg. Again it was Howard who talked to her in a whisper I couldn't understand. She nodded and pressed a concealed button on the upper drawer of a chest in which one might have suspected neatly stacked underwear; instead it held carefully labeled drugs. Howard took some speed, some hash for Dick and marijuana for me. He paid cash, as far as I could see, a horrendous sum, and the old lady closed the chest and went back to her chair in the corner, shoving the money under her breasts. She tinkled a bell and the man from outside the entrance came in. He moved a heavy cupboard away from the wall as easily as if it had been a matchbox. Behind it was a small door.

"Know if somebody called Doug is here?" I asked him.

No one had ever looked at me with such contempt. Not only his eyes, but his whole body expressed it—the way he

shrugged, the way his belly shook in a silent chuckle.
"Names don't mean anything here, bud."

As we walked through the door, a voice, it may have been
an old man's but it sounded more like a parrot's, croaked,
"God be with you. Enjoy yourself."

There was a long corridor with several doors opening from
it. In the first room psychedelic lights played a rainbow of
colors over a group of people dressed in white sheets, lying
on the ground. A sign read, STRICTLY NO ALCOHOL. In the
second, four young people were having intercourse. They
didn't even look up. Through a third door we walked into
what resembled a small hospital ward, with beds in a row
and all the curtains drawn around them for privacy. At the
far end was a basin with water dripping from a faucet and
an arrow pointing to the john.

"Jenny," Howard told me, "was a well-established prosti-
tute, but once past her prime, she came down all the way.
From Fifth Avenue to the Bowery."

"Hasn't she ever been raided?"

"Many times. But she keeps moving. And she pays high
for protection."

Some of the cubicles were larger than others. One could
have held ten people, another only one. Groups of young
and elderly men and girls were lying or sitting on the floor,
sharing their escape from reality or withdrawn into themselves. The stench of perspiration, sperm, urine, and drugs
was overpowering.

We took the right side first, Dick pushing the curtains
aside before he let me peer over his shoulder. Then we tried
the left. No sign of Doug. Howard went off to talk to Jenny
again and came back to tell us there were some private
rooms, past the arrow pointing to the john. Now I understood why he had paid so much for the drugs. We passed a
bend in the corridor and came out onto a wider passage. The
noise from the rooms on either side was deafening, as if
every percussion instrument in the world were being played

here. In the first room a woman in her fifties stood naked, splattering paint on a grimy wall. She smiled when she saw us. "Great, isn't it?"

"Far out," said Howard. "Whew!" And he closed the door.

In the second, a light was glaring from a strong spot, placed in one corner, a hi-fi was playing and couples were dancing cheek to cheek, the way people used to dance. A rat was feasting in a corner on cookies scattered carelessly on the floor. The third room was dark. Quiet. Dick shone his flashlight into it, and there, on a sagging couch, lay Doug.

"Leave me alone with him," I told Dick, "but stay close enough for your tape recorder to pick up what's being said."

I borrowed his flashlight and with its help found a candle on a crate next to the couch. I lit it. A few glassine bags, most of them empty, a box half filled with sugar cubes, a bottle with some solution. LSD I guessed, but I couldn't be sure because I knew too little about the stuff.

I sat down on the couch. He was half naked. He had rolled up his shirt under his head. His feet were bare, dirty, and red with cold. Every rib was showing in his thin body. There was no hair on his chest yet, just the shadow of down. Suddenly I felt unbelievably sorry for him. I put my hand on his shoulder and shook him gently. "Doug?"

"Sh," he said. "I'm not asleep." His voice sounded perfectly normal.

"It's time to go home," I said, and at that moment didn't think I had it in me to trick this thin, sad little boy into a confession.

"Home is here," he said. "Go away."

"Do you know who I am?"

He opened his eyes and sat up with a start, almost as if he had become aware only then of somebody's presence. "Sure I know. You're Mr. Wood. How did you get in? I locked the door."

"I found it open. Perhaps you forgot."

"Who are you?"

"You just recognized me. Tad. Tad Wood."

"And what are you doing here?"

"I've come to take you home."

"How did you know I was here?"

"Melinda . . ."

He interrupted me before I could go on. "You know, it's because of her I'm here."

He sank back, his eyes wide open but without any expression. A moment ago I'd thought that the effect from whatever he had taken had worn off, now I wasn't so sure. "Come on. Put on your shirt. Get up, and let's go home."

He didn't seem to hear me.

"Doug?"

"What is it?"

"Didn't you hear me? Didn't you hear what I said?"

"I wasn't aware you were talking to me."

"But I am. And I'm asking you to get up and put on your shirt and your sandals and come home with me."

"I'm not going home, that's for sure."

"If you don't want to go home, maybe we can find a boarding school where you'll feel at home."

"Shit!"

"Melinda will be home any day now."

This did something for him. His face lit up, not with joy though but with a light that was feverish—or so I preferred to think—rather than diabolical. "Well, now you're talking!"

I felt I had him, but instead of relief, I was filled with a terrible uneasiness. "Okay, then let's go."

"By all means. There's something I've got to tell her. And then I'll kill her."

"Kill Melinda? Why?"

"Because she's rotten. I almost killed you too, Mr. Wood, if you want to know."

"I do want to know. Why should you want to kill me?"

"Because at first thought it was you." He seemed to be

making preparations to leave, running his fingers through his long black hair, dirty now. When he had first let it grow, it had been enviably clean and silky. "Unfair," Melinda had said. "I know girls who'd give their eyeteeth to have hair like that."

"You thought it was me?"

"The guy who was screwing her."

"Whatever made you think that?"

"It was going on in your room, wasn't it? And after she'd told me she didn't want to have anything to do with me, she had better fish to fry. A real man. No balls, she said, meaning me. There's nothing wrong with my balls." He unzipped his pants. There wasn't. He zipped himself up again. "Let me tell you something, Mr. Wood, in case you're interested. I did it first when I was fourteen. But she wouldn't believe me."

"So she broke with you."

"Liar! I told her I wouldn't touch her with a ten-foot pole after I found out."

"Found out what?"

"Oh, it took time. First I wasted weeks spying on you. Followed you everywhere. When you went off on those long walks with her. Wondered why I didn't want to go along, didn't you? Well, I went along all right. I'm a good spy. Should join the CIA. They could do with a few." He laughed, a high-pitched laugh, almost like the bleating of a goat. "Makes you feel almighty. I've followed my father, too. He thinks nobody knows, but I do. Fucks his secretary twice a week. What a dog! Don't see how he can touch her."

He had turned away from me and was lying sideways, one filthy hand pawing the wall, as if he had forgotten his decision to come with me. "So now you want to kill Melinda."

"And I shall. It's not hard to kill. You want to tell me it's immoral? All this crap about morals. Who's got morals? Nobody has, and least of all Melinda. I know. I saw them together. In your room."

The sweat was breaking out on my face. "It's awfully

stuffy in here," I said. "I think I'd better open the window."

"You can't do that," he said. "Not if there's a light on."

I made my way to the window, and he pointed to the hooks fastened to the wooden shutters inside it. Then he blew out the candle and I threw the window open wide, breathing with relief the fresh cold air which came into the small hot room like an assault. But he didn't seem to approve of the interruption. Probably he had expected me to react more strongly to what he had revealed. He watched me come back to the couch, still with that bright evil look on his face. "I killed him, you know. The dirty old man. I was so fast, he didn't even have time to scream. A quick clean job."

His eyes were like the unseeing eyes of a drunk, yet he seemed to be looking straight at me. "You don't believe me?" The question had an undertone of exasperation. He took a switchblade from under his rolled up shirt and snapped it open. "Never without it," he said. "This is what I used on him. And you want to know something, and this is the pay-off—the dirty old man was a Justice of the Supreme Court of the U-ni-ted States of America!"

He rolled over on his back, laughing, no bleating goat but a man's roar.

"A Justice of the Supreme Court," he repeated, like an orator now. "I mean, how much higher can you go? And d'you know what I've been doing ever since? Lying here, lying there, taking this, taking that, trying to make up my mind to tell and make a splash or . . . You know they never put it in the papers, about his wig and the beard. Can you imagine where that left me? *So she doesn't even know!* I'm going to tell her. I'm going to be the one to tell her." He looked at me as if seeing me for the first time. "And not you, you goddamn bastard!"

I didn't see the knife flash; I only felt it entering between my ribs. I must have shouted, or moaned, anyway—the next moment Dick Corbett was there, and Detective Howard, trying to restrain the crazed kid. I could see them struggling in the powerful beam of Corbett's flashlight, but Doug tore loose. With one long stride he reached the window. For the eternity of a second he stood poised, his thin, naked chest glistening with sweat. "This should do it," he said, to nobody in particular, and dived head first through the window.

CHAPTER

TWENTY-SEVEN

FATHER CENCI CAME to the French Hospital early the next morning. He was sitting in a chair by the window, reading his breviary. I couldn't tell how long he had been waiting for me to wake up. I had slept soundly. The wound Doug had inflicted was more serious than I had thought. The knife had entered my right side between the third and fourth rib, penetrating the pleural space. The wound had been closed in emergency surgery, and I was to stay in the hospital for two weeks at least, and four more under medical care.

"Father Cenci. Why didn't you wake me? And how good of you to come right away."

"I came as soon as the hospital called me. And I've brought the envelope. I figured that was what you wanted."

"Would it be asking too much . . ." I had difficulty breathing because the right lung was not participating fully in the exchange of air. He noticed it and raised his hand. "Take it easy. I have time."

"I'd like you to go to the Chase Manhattan, the Fourteenth Street branch, and take out the contents of the safety box and burn them. Right there."

Before he left, I told him a little of what had happened,

and worst of all, how tormented I still was over the way I'd tricked Doug into his confession.

"I can understand you very well," he said. "Sometimes I find it almost beyond my powers to impose a sufficiently high penance on what is obviously a mortal sin. Especially with the young. Their conscience has not been sufficiently educated, or let us say, educated in the wrong direction. Today, for instance, children use a light meter, if they're going to take a picture, to get it right . . ."

"Nowadays most cameras have them built in," I said. "You don't have to bother any more to measure the light."

"You don't?" said Father Cenci. "Now that's too bad. Everything's made too easy for us. We rely less and less on study, and I don't mean in school. If only we could take an example from our inventions. It would be a good thing, perhaps, if parents and teachers, or the church, were to construct a light measure in a growing child . . . I mean now light in the broadest sense. The children of today have no measure, no measure at all."

A little later San Angelo came in. I knew him too well not to notice how upset he was and trying not to show it by speaking even more brusquely than usual. "Don't talk," he said, as I started to speak. "I know everything. Corbett called me. Thank God he and Howard got you to the hospital before police arrived. He gave me the tape of your conversation with Doug. From now on I'm going to handle everything. And don't feel too badly about the boy. There's no telling what the verdict might have been. He's better off dead, Tad, than in prison or a reformatory."

I tried to put Doug out of my mind, lying on that sagging couch at Jenny's, so pitifully thin and pale. The sunlight from outside fell on San Angelo's black hair, making it gleam. "Look for a black-haired man," Snipe had said. "I owe you an apology, San."

San Angelo took a cigar out of his breast-pocket, then, apparently in consideration of my condition, put it back again. And generous as he was, he laid his hand on mine for a second, establishing by the gesture the fact that he had forgiven me for my suspicion of him. "I wanted to kill Butworth," he said, "but I couldn't. You said once you could have understood it if I had, that in my place you'd have done the same thing. But you wouldn't have. No more than I did. And not because neither of us had the guts to ram a knife into his back. But you and I have grown up in a tradition that pretends to respect life. This new generation has become disillusioned by our hypocrisy. For Doug human life was no longer sacred. All that counted was good or evil, and these he saw quite clearly. The trouble starts when they take the law into their own inexperienced hands, with a violence and a hatred that is frightening."

Dusk fell early that afternoon, or so it seemed to me. By six it was quite dark. I hadn't heard from Caroline all day, and now she would be boarding her plane. It took some effort to recall that she hardly ever listened to the news, and today, with all the last-minute preparations for her trip, she wouldn't make an exception. Besides, it might not yet have been made public, and certainly I wouldn't have been mentioned.

I should have called her, as I had promised, but somehow I felt too weak to pick up the phone, to dial, to talk and explain. Then the phone rang, and when I heard her voice, I no longer felt weak.

"I'm sorry," she said, "to call only now. But I didn't know anything at all until Father Cenci reached me." And rapidly, so rapidly I could hardly follow, she explained that her phone had already been disconnected, and that she had been in and out all day, and that it was by pure chance that she had finally met up with the priest. "If I'm not the stupidest girl in the world . . . I should have guessed that you needed those damn photos to help . . ."

"I hoped you would," I said, interrupting her before she could mention any names. "Where are you?"

"At the airport, of course."

"Wearing what?"

"Wearing *what?*"

"I want to imagine you."

I could almost see her looking down at herself before she answered. "Blue denim slacks, a blue leather coat, and, yes, a blue beret. Knitted."

"Wear the same when you come back."

"Why?"

"I'll know what to look for in all that crowd when I come to pick you up."

And Caroline laughed.